FIFTY
FAMOUS FAIRY TALES

The
GOLDEN PRESS
Classics Library

FIFTY FAMOUS
FAIRY TALES

Illustrated by
ROBERT J. LEE

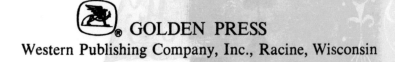

GOLDEN PRESS

Western Publishing Company, Inc., Racine, Wisconsin

Contents

Cinderella

ONCE UPON A TIME there lived a rich man who had a very beautiful daughter. The child's mother died, and after a time the man married a widow who had two daughters.

He thought she would make a good stepmother for his little girl, but the wedding was scarcely over when this stepmother began to treat the man's daughter unkindly. She was jealous because the girl was so much more beautiful than her own two daughters and had a much sweeter disposition. The girl was always so gentle and kind that it made the stepmother's two daughters seem even more disagreeable than they were, which was disagreeable enough.

The daughters, too, became envious of their stepsister, and they persuaded their mother to keep her working in the kitchen from morning till night, scrubbing and rubbing and doing all the hardest tasks. Each night when the girl's work was finished, she was so weary that she would sit right down in the chimney corner among the cinders. So the stepmother and the stepsisters began to call her Cinderella.

One day Cinderella heard her two stepsisters shouting and shrieking and acting altogether in such a dither that she was sure something unusual had happened. And so it had. The two stepsisters had been invited to a royal ball at the King's palace! The ball was to last three nights in a row and, most exciting of all, the King's son was to choose his bride from among the young ladies who were present.

The two stepsisters went out at once to buy the most gorgeous gowns they could find. When the first night of the ball came, they dressed themselves in all their finery and demanded that Cinderella curl their hair in the very latest fashion. Poor Cinderella curled their hair, and nicely, too; brought their gloves and fans; polished their slippers; and fetched and carried for them, upstairs and down, till at last when they were ready to go, Cinderella was completely worn out.

When the door shut behind them, the poor girl sank down on her stool among the cinders and wept.

"Oh, I wish I could go, too," she sobbed.

"Tears, tears, tears!" said a soft voice. "Dry your eyes, child."

Cinderella looked up and saw a little old woman with a tall, pointed hat on her head and a golden wand in her hand.

"Who are you?" asked Cinderella.

"I am your fairy godmother," said the little old woman. "Because you have always been good and gentle, I shall grant your wish. You may go to the ball, if you will do exactly as I tell you. Run out to the garden and fetch me the biggest pumpkin you can find."

Cinderella did not see how a pumpkin could help her get to the ball, but she did as she was told and soon returned with a fine big one.

The little old woman touched it with her magic wand. Lo and behold! The pumpkin turned into a golden coach! Next she took six mice out of the mousetrap and changed each one into a sleek gray pony.

"Bring me a fat rat from the cellar," said the godmother. When Cinderella did so, the rat was turned into a handsome coachman in full livery.

Then the fairy godmother said, "Now run out to the garden and lift up the watering can near the fence. Under it you will find six lizards which you must catch and bring to me." These were no sooner brought than, with a touch of the wand, they were turned into six footmen, who immediately jumped up behind the coach!

"There!" cried the godmother. "Off you go!" But Cinderella looked down at her soiled, ragged dress and her eyes filled with tears.

"Tears, tears, tears," said the godmother. "Dry your eyes, child." And she waved her wand. Immediately Cinderella's rags and tatters were changed into a beautiful dress as blue as the sky and covered with jewels. Her shoes became the daintiest pair of glass slippers ever seen.

"Now," said the little old woman as she helped the happy girl into the coach. "Have a good time, but remember this: you must not stay one minute after midnight. If you do, your coach will become a pumpkin again; your horses, mice; your footmen, lizards; your coachman, a rat. And your beautiful dress will turn into rags."

Cinderella promised she would leave the ball before midnight. She thanked her fairy godmother many times, and drove off.

When her golden coach drew up at the palace, the news quickly spread that an unknown princess had come to the ball. The King's son greeted her and was so delighted with her beauty that he promptly asked her for the next dance. She was so graceful that everyone in the room turned to admire her, and the Prince scarcely left her side all evening.

He had just gone to bring her a dish of sweetmeats when Cinderella noticed that it was nearly midnight. She quickly slipped away and returned home in her golden carriage. Her fairy godmother was waiting for her, and Cinderella told her what a wonderful time she had had, and how the Prince had begged her to come back the next evening. The little old woman was quite pleased and promised Cinderella that she should go to the palace again.

The following evening, as soon as the two stepsisters had gone, the fairy godmother appeared. She gave Cinderella a gown as sweet and dainty as a pink rosebud, and off Cinderella went. The Prince was so delighted to see her that he would dance with no one else. But shortly before midnight, she darted away from him and vanished so quickly that he could not follow her. The godmother was pleased because Cinderella had remembered to come home on time and promised her she could go the third night, also.

The next evening, Cinderella's dress was as golden as sunshine. She made such a charming picture with her golden curls and golden dress that a murmur of admiration went through the crowd as she entered the ballroom. The Prince, who had refused to dance until she arrived, came to her at once, and it was easy to see that he was very much in love with her.

The Prince was so charming that Cinderella forgot all about the time until the clock began to strike twelve. She jumped up and fled from the room. The startled Prince raced after her. She managed to escape him, but in her haste she lost one of her glass slippers. Just as the last stroke of twelve died away, she reached the courtyard. In a twinkling, the beautiful princess was just a shabby little cinder girl again. The golden coach was nothing but a pumpkin, and the coachman and footmen were no longer there. Cinderella reached home quite out of breath, and nothing remained of her lovely costume but one little glass slipper.

When her two sisters returned home, they told Cinderella all about the mysterious princess who had fled from the ball. Cinderella's heart beat faster when she heard how the Prince had picked up the lost glass slipper and had looked at it fondly all the rest of the evening. But she said not a word.

The next morning, the news went around that the Prince would marry the maiden whose foot exactly fitted the glass slipper, for it was so tiny that he was sure only the mysterious princess could wear it. When the stepsisters heard this, each one was sure that she could squeeze her foot into the slipper, somehow.

A messenger was sent from house to house with the slipper, and all the young ladies tried to put it on. But they tried in vain, for it would not fit.

At last the two sisters had their turn. They tried so hard to squeeze into the slipper that their bones cracked. The messenger was about to leave when Cinderella said, "Please, may I try to put on the slipper?"

"You!" shrieked the stepsisters. "Go back to the kitchen where you belong!"

But the messenger said that the Prince had given orders that every maiden was to try the slipper, and he handed it to Cinderella. Of course the slipper fitted her perfectly, and when she pulled the mate from her pocket, the sisters and the stepmother were speechless with amazement. At that instant the fairy godmother appeared, waved her wand over Cinderella, and clothed her again in the beautiful golden dress.

The stepsisters threw themselves at her feet and begged forgiveness for treating her so badly. Cinderella, who was as good as she was beautiful, forgave them at once and asked them to love her always.

Then the messenger took Cinderella to the palace, and the Prince asked her to marry him without delay. A few days later, the wedding took place. Cinderella became a real Princess and lived happily with the handsome Prince, ever afterward.

Jack the Giant Killer

MANY YEARS AGO, in the time of King Arthur, there lived a giant named Cormoran who was the terror of all the country of Cornwall. He was eighteen feet tall and at least nine feet around the middle and he had a tremendous appetite. He would kill a half-dozen cows and as many sheep and pigs, and carry them all home for one meal.

All the countryfolk were greatly alarmed, for if this went on for long, the whole of Cornwall would be laid bare. They tried hiding their farm animals, but then the giant Cormoran carried off the people themselves for food. So the countryfolk let him take their cattle as he pleased, for no one dared fight the eighteen-foot giant.

Now at this same time there lived in Cornwall a young boy named Jack, who determined to slay the giant. Since he knew he could not kill him by force, he made up his mind to kill him by trickery.

So one night Jack set off alone and went boldly up the mountain where the giant lived. He took with him a dark lantern, a hunting horn, an ax, and a shovel. In the middle of the path that led to the giant's cave, Jack dug a pit twenty feet deep and twenty feet wide and twenty feet long. Then he covered the pit with branches and dirt. When the hole was thus cleverly hidden, Jack took out his horn, blew a loud blast, and then quickly hid behind a tree.

The giant started from his sleep, roaring with anger.

"Who dares to wake me so early in the morning?" he bellowed. Jumping up from his bed, he rushed out of the cave, shouting furiously.

"Whoever you are, I'll boil you for breakfast!"

Still roaring, the giant plunged on down the path, hunting his tormentor. Suddenly he stepped on the covering of the pit. Down he fell! Jack sprang from his hiding place, clouted the giant on the head with the ax, and that was the end of the giant, Cormoran.

The countryfolk sang and danced for joy at the giant's death. They gave Jack a wonderful sword, and from then on he was known from one end of the country to the other as Jack the Giant Killer.

Of course with a name like that, Jack was the enemy of every evil giant alive. It was not long till another giant heard of him and swore to take revenge on him. Jack knew that he must kill this Welsh giant or he would be killed himself. Since trickery had worked so well the first time, Jack wanted to try it again. But of course he couldn't use the same trick. So he decided to visit the Welsh giant (who had never seen Jack and would not recognize him) and see what trick he could think of to do away with the evil fellow.

When he came to the giant's castle, Jack marched up to the door, knocked politely, and asked the giant to give him a night's lodging. The giant seemed cordial enough and invited Jack to come in, but there was a certain sly look in the giant's eye that Jack didn't like. And when Jack saw the pile of human bones in the giant's fireplace, he knew he would have to think fast or his own would soon be among them.

On the table before the fireplace was a dish with four gallons of mush and milk in it. The giant set another of these huge dishes before Jack.

"Get away with this, if you can," he said. Not wishing the giant to think it was too much for him, Jack ate what he could and secretly poured the rest into a leather bag he had hidden under his shirt.

When the dishes were empty, Jack challenged the giant to a contest of skill.

"Faugh!" sneered the giant. "Whatever you do, I can do much better."

"So?" said Jack. "Then do this." And he drew out his sword and split open the leather bag as if it were his stomach. Out tumbled all the mush and milk.

The giant, not to be outdone by any ordinary man, slit his own stomach and, of course, fell to the floor dead. Then Jack left the castle and made his way to King Arthur's court. There he lived for some time.

One day Jack learned that the King's son was very unhappy because the Princess he wished to marry had been bewitched by the giant Galligantua and carried off to his castle in the form of a deer.

Of course Jack had no choice but to go to the giant's castle in search of the Princess. After traveling a long time he came to a castle guarded by two ferocious monsters with heads of eagles and the bodies of lions. Jack slipped into the invisible cloak he had brought along and passed by the monsters unnoticed. When he entered the castle the first thing that caught his eye was a gold hunting horn hanging on the wall. Beneath it were the words:

"Whoever doth this trumpet blow
Shall cause the giant's overthrow."

Jack seized the trumpet and blew a great blast. The terrible monsters fell down dead, and suddenly Jack found himself surrounded by a throng of animals big and little.

Among them was a beautiful, sad-eyed deer. She looked at Jack and then walked away. Jack followed her and soon found himself in the room where Galligantua slept. Quick as breath, Jack drew his sword and cut off the giant's head. As he did so the deer became the princess, and all the other animals became their human selves again.

Shouting and singing for joy, they all marched back to the court of King Arthur. The Prince and the Princess were married, and Jack himself married the daughter of a duke. King Arthur gave him a fine castle and rich farmlands as a reward, and there Jack and his wife lived in great contentment and happiness for many a year.

The Six Travelers

THERE WAS ONCE a soldier who had served bravely in the army, but when the war came to an end he received his discharge and a miserable three farthings as salary for all his years of service.

"Lackaday! I don't like this," he said to himself. "If I find the right people, I shall make the King give me all the treasures of the kingdom." And thumping his fists with anger, the soldier stamped off. By and by he met a man who had just uprooted six trees as if they were stalks of corn. The soldier marveled at his strength and asked him to travel with him.

"That I will do and gladly," replied the man, "but first I shall take this bundle of firewood home to my mother." Taking up one of the trees, he wound it around the other five, and raising the bundle to his shoulder, took it away. Soon he returned and said, "We two shall get along in the world!"

They had not gone far before they came upon a hunter who was kneeling on one knee aiming with his gun. The soldier asked him what he was going to shoot, and he replied, "Two miles from here a fly is sitting on the branch of an oak tree, and I wish to shoot out its left eye."

"Oh, come with us," said the soldier, "for if we three are together, we shall surely get on in the world." The huntsman consented and went with them.

Soon they saw seven windmills whose sails were going round at a rattling pace, although there was no wind. At this sight the soldier said, "I wonder what drives these mills, for there is no breeze!" They went on, but they had not gone more than two miles when they saw a man holding one nostril while he blew out of the other.

"My good fellow, what are you doing?" asked the soldier.

"Didn't you see seven windmills two miles from here?" replied the man. "I am blowing to make their sails go round."

"Oh, then, come with us," said the soldier, "for, if four people like us travel together, we shall soon get on in the world." So the blower got up and accompanied them.

In a short while, they met another man standing on one leg. The other leg was unbuckled and lying by his side. The soldier said, "You have done this, no doubt, to rest yourself?"

"Yes," replied the man, "I am a runner, and in order that I may not spring along too quickly I have unbuckled one of my legs. When I wear both, I go as fast as a bird."

"Well, then, come with us," said the soldier. "Five such fellows as we are will soon get up in the world."

The five travelers went on together and soon met a man who had a hat which he wore over one ear. The soldier said to him, "Manners! Manners! Don't hang your hat on one side like that! You look like a simpleton!"

"I dare not do otherwise," replied the other, "for, if I set my hat straight, a frost so sharp will come that the birds in the sky will freeze and fall dead on the ground."

"Then come with us," said the soldier, "for it is odd if six fellows like us cannot quickly get up in the world."

These six companions came to a city where the King had proclaimed that whoever would win a race with his daughter should become her husband, but if he lost the race, he would also lose his head. The soldier heard of this and asked that his servant be allowed to run for him. The King agreed but said the soldier as well as the servant would lose his life if the race were lost. The soldier agreed and bade his runner buckle on his other leg to make sure of winning.

The race was from the palace gate to a distant mountain spring. The first to bring back water from the spring would be the winner. Accordingly the runner and the Princess each received a cup, and the race was started. The Princess ran with the speed of a young deer, but in less than a minute the runner had passed her and was out of sight. In a short time he came to the spring and, filling his cup, he started back. He had not gone very far when, feeling tired, he lay down to take a nap.

Meanwhile, the Princess had arrived at the spring, and was returning with her cup of water. When she came upon her opponent lying asleep, her eyes sparkled wickedly; and emptying his cup, she ran on still faster.

All would now have been lost if the huntsman had not been standing at the castle watching the runners with his sharp eyes. When he saw what the Princess had done, he loaded his gun and shot so cleverly that he carried away the rock under the runner's head. This awakened the runner. Jumping up, he found his cup empty and the Princess far ahead. However, he did not lose courage, but once again ran to the spring and, filling his cup, started back. He ran so fast that he passed the Princess and won the race with a good ten minutes to spare.

The King and his daughter were disgusted that a common soldier should win a princess for a bride, and they plotted how they could get rid of him and his companions. At last the King said, "Do not distress yourself, my dear. I know a way to prevent their return."

Then he called to the six travelers and led them into a
room with a floor of iron, doors of iron, and windows
guarded with iron bars. In the room there was a table set
with choice delicacies. The King invited them to enter and
refresh themselves. As soon as they were inside, he locked
and bolted all the doors. That done, he called the cook and
commanded him to keep a fire lighted beneath the room
until the iron was red-hot. The cook obeyed, and the six
companions sitting at the table soon began to feel quite hot.
As they grew hotter and hotter, they tried to leave the room
and found the doors and windows all locked. Then they
realized that the wicked King meant to roast them alive.

"This is where I come in," cried the man with the hat.
So saying, he put his hat on straight. Immediately such a
frost fell that all the heat disappeared.

Two hours passed. The King thought the six unwanted
guests must be roasted, and he opened the door and went
in to see them. But as the door was opened, all six stood
shivering before him and asked to come out to warm themselves, for, they said, the cold in the room was so intense
that all the dishes of food were frozen.

In great anger, the King went down to the cook. He
asked why his instructions had not been obeyed. The cook
pointed to the roaring fire and said, "There is heat enough
there, I should think!" The King was obliged to admit there
was, and he saw that he would not be able to get rid of his
visitors in the way he had planned.

Again the King began to wonder how he could rid himself of his guests. Finally, he summoned the soldier and
said, "Will you take money, and give up your right to my
daughter? If so, you may have as much as you can carry."

"Well, my lord," replied the man, "give me as much as
my servant can carry, and you are welcome to keep your
daughter with you."

This answer pleased the King, and the soldier said that he would send his servant to fetch the sum of money in fourteen days. During that time he had tailors make him a gigantic sack. As soon as it was ready, the strong man who had uprooted the trees took the sack and carried it to the King.

At the sight of him the King was filled with dismay and said, "What a powerful fellow this must be!" And he sighed heavily, for he saw that he would have to give up much more gold than he had expected. The King, first of all, had a ton of gold brought. Sixteen ordinary men were required to lift it, but the strong man, taking it up with one hand, shoved it into the sack, saying. "Why don't you bring more at a time? This scarcely covers the bottom of the sack."

So the King ordered one wagonload of gold after the other till seven thousand wagons all laden with gold had

been brought. And all these the strong man pushed into his
sack. Still it was not full, and the strong man offered to take
whatever was brought, if it would but fill his sack. So they
brought cups and plates and jewels and silk and fine furs
until at last the man said, "Well, I must make an end to
this, and, besides, if one's sack is not quite full, why, it can
be tied up so much easier!" So saying, he hoisted the sack
upon his back, and he went away.

When the King saw this one man carrying away all the
riches of his kingdom, he became extremely angry and
ordered his soldiers to pursue the man and bring him back.
Two regiments on horseback took after the man, who by
now had met his companions. The soldiers soon overtook
the six travelers and shouted out to them, "You are our
prisoners! Lay down the sack of gold!"

The strong man did not answer, but the blower spoke
up.

"What is that you are saying?" asked the blower. "You
will make us prisoners? Well, first you will have a dance in
the air!" So saying, he held one nostril, and with the other
blew the two regiments away into the sky. One sergeant
begged for mercy. As he was a brave fellow undeserving of
such disgrace, the blower sent a gentle puff after him and
brought him back without harming him. Then he was sent
back to the King with a message that, whatever number
of soldiers he might send, all would be blown into the air
like the first lot.

When the King heard this message, he said, "Let the
fellows go; I made a bargain and I must put up with it."

So the six companions took home all the wealth of the kingdom and, sharing it with one another, lived contentedly all
the rest of their days.

Hansel and Gretel

ONCE LONG AGO a poor woodcutter lived at the edge of a large forest with his two children, a boy named Hansel and a girl named Gretel, and their stepmother. Now it happened that there was a great scarcity of food in the land and the poor woodcutter could not get enough to feed his family. One evening when Hansel and Gretel were in bed, the man sighed and said to his wife, "What will become of us? How can we feed my children when we haven't anything to eat ourselves?"

"There is only one thing to do," the stepmother answered. "We shall lead them into the thickest part of the forest tomorrow, build them a fire and give each of them a small piece of bread. Then we shall leave them. They will not be able to find their way home again, and we shall be freed of them."

"No, wife," he replied, "I could never do that. How could you be cruel enough to leave the children in the forest for the wild beasts to tear to pieces?"

But she said it was better to let them die suddenly than to watch them slowly starve to death, and she gave him no peace until he finally consented to leave Hansel and Gretel in the woods as she had suggested.

However, the children had overheard all that was said, for they were so hungry that they had not been able to sleep.

Gretel wept bitterly, and said to Hansel, "What will become of us?"

"Don't cry, Gretel," he said. "I shall take care of you."

When their parents fell asleep, Hansel got up and slipped out the back door. The moon shone brightly, and the white pebbles that lay on the path glittered like silver coins. He filled his pocket with them and then going back to Gretel, he said, "Go to sleep, dear sister. God will not forsake us."

Early the next morning, the wife called to the children.

"Get up, you lazy things; we are going into the forest to chop wood." She gave them each a piece of bread, saying, "This is for your dinner. Do not eat it until noon."

Gretel took the bread in her apron, for Hansel's pocket was full of pebbles. When they had gone a little distance, Hansel stood still and looked back at the house. After he had repeated this several times, his father called back, "Hansel, what are you looking at, and why do you lag behind?"

"Why, Father," said Hansel, "I am looking at my white cat sitting on the roof of the house. He is trying to say good-bye."

"That is not a cat," said his stepmother. "It is only the sun shining on the white chimney."

Hansel had not been looking at a cat at all. Every time he stopped to look back he had dropped a pebble out of his pocket. When they were deep in the forest, their father told the children to gather wood and build a fire. Then, as the flames burned high, the wife said, "Now, you children lie down close to the fire and rest yourselves. We are going to chop wood. When we are ready to go home, I shall come and fetch you."

Hansel and Gretel sat down near the fire, and after a while they ate their bread. They could hear the blows of an ax, so they thought their father was near. However, it was not an ax, but a branch which he had bound to an old tree,

being blown to and fro. The two children waited a long
while, and at last they fell asleep.

When they awakened it was quite dark, and Gretel began
to cry.

"How are we going to get out of the woods?"

Hansel comforted her by saying, "Wait a little while until
the moon comes up. Then we shall quickly find the way."

In a little while the moon came up. Hansel, taking his
sister's hand, followed the pebbles which glittered like new-
coined silver pieces and showed them the path. All night
long they walked, and at daybreak they came to their father's
house.

They knocked at the door. When the stepmother opened
it and saw Hansel and Gretel, she exclaimed, "You wicked
children! Why did you sleep so long in the forest? We
thought that you were never coming home." But their
father was happy to see them, for he had been sad at heart
over leaving them.

But the crops were no better than before, and food was
still scarce. Once more the stepmother nagged the woodcutter to take the children into the forest and leave them.
The children overheard this conversation, also, and as soon
as the older people were asleep, Hansel got up in order to go
outside for some pebbles. But his stepmother had locked
the door.

Early the next morning the stepmother woke them and
gave them a small slice of bread. On the way to the woods
Hansel crumbled his and stopped every now and then to
drop a crumb.

"Hansel, why do you stop and look about?" asked his
father.

"I am looking at my little dove," answered Hansel. "He
is nodding good-bye to me."

"That is no dove," said his stepmother. "It is only the

sun shining on the chimney." But Hansel kept dropping crumbs as he went along.

The wife led the children into the deepest part of the woods where they had never been before. Making an immense fire, she said to them, "Sit here and rest awhile, and if you feel tired sleep a bit. We are going into the forest to chop wood. When it is time, we'll come and fetch you."

After they had eaten their bread, the two children went to sleep, and when they awoke it was dark. Hansel comforted his sister by saying, "Wait, Gretel. When the moon comes out we'll be able to see the crumbs of bread that I dropped, and they will show us the way home."

The moon soon shone bright, but the children could not see any crumbs, for the birds had picked them all up. Hansel kept assuring Gretel that they would soon find their way, but they walked the whole night and the next day, and still they did not get out of the forest. They became very hungry, for they had nothing to eat but a few wild berries.

Hansel and Gretel walked on and on, but they only got deeper and deeper into the forest. Suddenly they saw a beautiful snow-white bird sitting on a bough. The bird was singing so sweetly that they stood still and listened. When it spread its wings and flew off, the children followed till it reached a cottage and perched upon the roof. As Hansel and Gretel drew near, they saw that the cottage was made of gingerbread, the roof of cakes and the windowpanes were of sugar candy so clear you could see through it.

"Oh! Oh! Oh!" cried Hansel. "What a glorious feast! I shall eat a piece of the roof and you can eat some of the window."

Reaching up, Hansel broke off a bit of the roof to see how it tasted, and Gretel began to nibble at the window. Then a voice called out, "Tip-tap, tip-tap. At my window who doth rap?"

The children answered, "Wind of the air, breezes fair," and went right on eating.

Suddenly the door opened and a very old woman came out. Hansel and Gretel were so startled that they dropped what they had in their hands. The old woman said in a kindly voice, "Ah, you dear children, what has brought you here? Come into the house and eat all you wish." Then she took them both by the hand and led them into her cottage.

The old woman was very kind to them. But though her voice sounded gentle and her words were sweet, she was really a wicked witch. She had built the gingerbread house to attract children so that she might kill and eat them.

The next morning before the children awakened, the old witch went to look at them. Seeing their chubby red cheeks, she mumbled to herself, "That will be a good bite." She took Hansel and shut him up in a little cage with a lattice door, and although he screamed loudly it was of no use. Then she shook Gretel until she awakened and said, "Get up, you lazy thing, and fetch some water to cook something for your brother, who must remain in that cage and get fat. When he is fat enough, I shall eat him." Gretel began to cry but it was no use, for the old witch made her do as she wished. So a nice meal was cooked for Hansel, and Gretel got nothing but an old crab claw.

Every morning the old witch went to the cage and said, "Hansel, stretch out your finger so that I may see if you are getting fat." Each time clever Hansel stretched out a bone instead. The old witch, whose sight was very bad, thought that it was his finger and wondered why he did not get fat. When four weeks had passed and Hansel still seemed quite lean, she lost all her patience and could wait no longer. In a fit of temper she called out, "Gretel, get the oven heated. This morning I shall cook Hansel, fat or lean."

There was nothing for Gretel to do but make a fire to

heat the oven. When the witch thought the oven should be hot enough, she pushed Gretel up to it and said, "Creep in, and see if it is hot enough." She intended to shut the door when Gretel got into the oven and so roast her, too.

Gretel guessed her thoughts, and said, "I don't know how to do it. How shall I get in?"

"You stupid goose," said the witch. "The opening is big enough. See, I could get in myself!" And she got up and put her head into the oven. As soon as she did this, Gretel gave her a push, so that the old witch fell right in. Then Gretel shut the iron door and fastened it tight.

As soon as she found the witch's keys, she ran to the cage and called, "Hansel, we are saved! The witch is in the oven!"

Hansel sprang out when the door opened. Now that there was no one to fear, the children searched the witch's house and found chests full of pearls and precious stones in every corner. Hansel filled his pockets and Gretel took as many as she could carry in her apron. Then they started out through the forest to find their way home again.

When they had walked about two hours, they came to a lake. "We cannot get over," said Hansel. "There is no bridge."

"There is no boat either," said Gretel, "but there swims a white duck. I shall ask her to help us over." So she sang:

> "Little duck, good little duck,
>   Gretel and Hansel before you stand,
>   There is neither boat nor bridge,
>   Take us back to your land."

The good duck came and took them to the other side. They did not walk much farther before they saw their father's house at the edge of the forest. They began to run, and, bursting into the house, they saw their father. They flung their arms about him, and he kissed them for joy at their return.

The woodcutter had not had one happy minute since he had left his children in the forest. The wicked stepmother was dead, and so now he was free to love his own dear children again.

"I'm a poor man but a happy one," he said.

Then Gretel shook her apron, and the pearls and precious stones rolled on the floor, while Hansel drew one handful of gems after the other out of his pocket.

The precious stones were worth a great deal of money, and Hansel and Gretel and their father never again wanted for anything.

The Dwarfs

ONCE UPON A TIME a rich King had three beautiful daughters. About his castle was a wonderful orchard in which all kinds of trees grew. The King had given warning that whoever should pluck and eat an apple from a certain tree would disappear a hundred feet into the ground. When autumn came, the apples on this tree looked so red and juicy that the three Princesses longed to taste them. Every day they went to the tree to see if any of the fruit had fallen. But the wind blew none down, and the Princesses dared not pluck any because of the King's warning.

One day the youngest of the three daughters said to her sisters, "Our father loves us so much that he will never cause us to disappear underground. He meant that warning only for strangers." So she plucked an apple. The other two sisters shared it with her, but as soon as they had eaten it, all three sank down below the earth.

By and by the King sent for his daughters, but they were nowhere to be found. At length, when his servants had searched the palace and grounds and could find no trace of them, the King had it proclaimed throughout the country that whoever should bring back a Princess could take her as a bride. Thereupon great numbers of young men set out in search of the royal maidens.

Among others there went out three huntsmen, who were

brothers. After traveling for eight days, they came to a large castle in which every room was splendidly furnished. In one room they found a large table and all manner of delicious food. Every dish was steaming hot and seemed fresh from the kitchen, yet nowhere did they hear or see anyone.

Since no one came, they ate what they liked. Afterward they agreed that one of them should remain in the castle each day and take his ease while the two others sought the Princesses. To decide who was to stay, they drew lots, and it fell to the share of the eldest to stay at the castle the first day.

About noon a little dwarf brought in roast meat which he cut in small pieces. While he held some out to the huntsman, he let one piece fall, and the dwarf asked the eldest brother to pick it up.

"Pick it up yourself!" said the eldest brother rudely. The dwarf did so, and as he bent over the brother kicked him, saying, "That will teach you who is servant and who is master."

The next day the second huntsman remained at the castle, and the dwarf dropped the meat as before. The second huntsman was as rude as his brother, and the dwarf went away shaking his fist.

The third day the youngest brother remained, and the dwarf dropped the meat as usual and asked the youth to pick it up.

"Gladly," said the youth, "for you have given us fine service." And he leaned over to do so.

Whereupon the little dwarf served him a meal twice as fine as any he had ever served before. Then the dwarf said, "You have done me a favor. Now I'll do you one. I will tell you how to find the King's daughters."

The little man explained that he was an underground

dwarf, and that there were more than a thousand like him. He also warned the huntsman that his two older brothers would try to trick him. Therefore, if he wanted to get the Princesses he must go alone. He must take with him his hunting knife and a great basket in which to let himself down into the well where the Princesses were kept. In this well he would find three rooms. In each of these was a Princess, guarded by a dragon. Each dragon had many heads and could be killed only by having its heads cut off. As soon as the dwarf had said all this, he disappeared.

In the evening the two older brothers returned and asked the youngest how he had passed the time.

"Oh, very well indeed," he replied. "At noon a dwarf came in and told me how to find the Princesses. They are in the well on the top of the hill."

The older brothers didn't believe him, but they thought they might as well search in one place as another. So the next morning all three brothers went up the hill to the well. They drew lots to see who should descend into the well first.

The lot fell, as before, to the eldest. He went down, taking a bell with him to ring as a signal when he wanted to come up again. As soon as he caught a glimpse of a dragon, this eldest brother rang his bell furiously. When he was drawn up, the second brother took his place and went down, but he quickly rang to be pulled up again.

The youngest brother's turn came next. He allowed himself to be let down to the very bottom of the well, and there, getting out of the basket, he marched boldly up to the first door with his drawn knife in his hand. Inside he heard a dragon snoring loudly. Carefully opening the door, he saw a Princess sitting within. The sleeping dragon lay with his nine heads on her lap.

Quickly the young huntsman raised his knife and cut off

the nine heads. Immediately the Princess jumped up and kissed him, and gave him her golden necklace for a reward.

Next he found the second Princess, who had a seven-headed dragon by her side. The young huntsman killed this beast also, and then went on to the youngest Princess. She was guarded by a four-headed dragon, and he destroyed it as he had the others. The three sisters embraced and kissed him till he thought he would be smothered. So he rang the bell very loudly to signal that he was ready to come up.

When the basket came down, he put each Princess in by turn, and let them be drawn up. As the basket descended for him, he remembered the dwarf's warning that his brothers would try to trick him. So he picked up a huge stone and put it in the basket instead of getting in himself. Just as the brothers had drawn it halfway up, they cut the cord at the top, and the basket with the stone in it clattered to the bottom. The two huntsmen thought they had rid themselves of the youngest brother, and they threatened to kill the three Princesses unless they promised never to tell their father who had truly rescued them. Then they went to the King and demanded the two eldest Princesses for their wives.

Meanwhile, the youngest brother was wandering sadly about underground and thought he would have to die there. All at once he saw a flute on the wall.

"Ah, me," he thought to himself, "what good can this be here? No one could be happy enough to sing or dance in this place." Up and down, to and fro, he walked until the floor was worn smooth.

At last he decided to make the best of things, and so he took the flute and blew three notes on it. Instantly three dwarfs appeared. He blew a little longer, and each note brought another dwarf, until at last the room was quite filled with the little men. They all asked what he wished, and he told them that he wanted to go up on earth again. Immediately, each dwarf seized a hair of the young huntsman's head, and up they flew with him until they landed him at the edge of the well.

As soon as he was safe on his legs again, he set out for the royal palace, and arrived there just as the weddings of the Princesses were about to be celebrated. He hurried up to the room where the King sat with his three daughters. They were so overcome by the sight of him that they fainted away. Immediately the King ordered the newcomer to be put in prison, for he thought the young huntsman had surely done the Princesses some injury. As soon as the Princesses had recovered, they begged their father to free the youth. He asked them the reason, but they wept bitterly and said they had promised not to tell him.

"Well, then," said the King, who suspected some evil trickery, "tell the oven. You didn't promise anything about that."

Then he slipped outside and listened at the keyhole while the youngest Princess told the oven the story. When the King heard the truth, he ordered the two wicked brothers to be hanged, but he gave his youngest daughter in marriage to the Princesses' true rescuer.

The Poor Man and the Rich Man

IN OLDEN TIMES angels often took the form of men and walked the earth. While one of these was wandering about, night came upon him before he had found shelter. At last he saw down the road ahead of him two houses standing opposite one another; one was large and handsome, while the other was miserably poor. The angel decided to ask for lodging in the large house, since it would be less burdensome for a rich man to entertain a guest. He knocked, and the rich man, peering out the window, asked the stranger what he sought.

The angel replied, "I seek a night's lodging."

Then the rich man looked scornfully at the stranger's ragged clothes and shook his head, saying, "I cannot take you in. If I sheltered everyone who knocks at my door, I might soon be a beggar myself! Find shelter in some other house."

And he banged the window and locked it. The good angel immediately turned his back upon the large house and went over to the little house. Here he had scarcely knocked when the door was opened. The poor man took one look at the stranger and said, "Come in. Come in. Stay here tonight; it is quite dark, and you can go no farther today."

This reception pleased the angel very much. The wife of the poor man also bade him welcome. Holding out her

hand she said, "Make yourself at home, good sir. Though
we do not have much, we will gladly share it with you."
Then she put some potatoes in the coals, and while they
roasted she milked her goat. When the table was laid, the
good angel sat down and ate with the poor couple. The
coarse food tasted good, because such a warm welcome went
with it. After they had finished eating, the wife called her
husband aside and said, "Let us sleep on straw tonight and
let this poor wanderer have our bed. He has been walking
all day, and is doubtless tired."

The good angel at first refused to take the bed, but at
last yielded to their entreaties and lay down on the soft
feather mattress while they made a straw couch upon the
floor.

The next morning the couple arose early and cooked their

guest a breakfast of the best that they had. When the angel finished eating, he prepared to set out again. As he stood in the doorway, he turned around and said to his hosts, "Because you are so good and generous, you may wish three times and each time I will grant what you desire."

The poor man replied, "Ah, what more can I wish for than eternal happiness, and that we two, so long as we live, may have health, and strength, and our daily bread. For the third thing I do not know what to wish."

"Would you like a new house in place of this old one?"

"Oh, yes," said the man, "if I may keep it in this spot, it would be welcome."

The last wish was fulfilled at once, and the old house became a new red-brick cottage. Then giving the couple his blessing, the angel went along down the road.

Shortly thereafter the rich man arose. He looked out of his window and saw a handsome new house of red brick standing where the old hut had been.

"Come and look!" he called to his wife.

The wife was as curious as her husband and went across the road at once and asked the poor man what had happened. He told the story of the wanderer and the three wishes he had granted. When the man had finished his tale, the rich man's wife ran home and told her husband.

"Ah! Had I only known it!" he exclaimed. "The stranger came here first, but I sent him away."

"Hurry, then!" cried his wife. "Mount your horse, and perhaps you may overtake the man. Tell him you meant to let him stay. Then you may ask three wishes for yourself."

The rich man followed this advice, and soon overtook the good angel. He begged him not to think ill of him, saying that he had gone to get the key for the door, and returned to find the wanderer gone. If only the angel would come back, he was welcome to stay. The angel promised that he would stop at the rich man's house on his return. Then the rich man asked if he might not have three wishes as his neighbor had.

"Yes," said the angel, "you may, but it will not be good for you, and it would be better if you did not wish."

But the rich man was sure he wanted the wishes. So the angel said, "Ride home, and your wishes will be granted."

The rich man was satisfied and as he rode homeward, he began to consider what he should wish. While he was thinking, he let his reins fall loose, and his horse stumbled so that the man nearly fell. "You dumb beast!" he cried out. "I wish you would break your neck!" He had no sooner said this than the horse fell to the ground and never moved again. Thus the rich man's first wish was fulfilled.

The rich man, being thrifty by nature, would not leave

the saddle behind. He cut it off, slung it over his back, and traveled on by foot. "I still have two wishes," he thought to himself, and so was comforted.

As he walked slowly homeward, the sun became very hot. The saddle hurt his back, and besides, he had not yet decided what to wish for next. "Even if I should wish for all the riches in the world," he said to himself, "something else will occur to me later. I must manage to make a wish so that nothing at all shall remain for me to wish for."

As he walked along the sun grew hotter, and the saddle rubbed his back until it was as sore as a burn. Then he thought of how his wife sat comfortably at home in a cool room. This thought angered him and, without knowing it, he said aloud, "I wish she were sitting on this saddle, and couldn't get off."

As soon as he spoke these words, the saddle disappeared from his back, and he realized that his second wish had been fulfilled. Cursing himself for a fool, he hurried home determined to lock himself in his room to consider his last wish. But when he arrived home, he found his wife sitting on the saddle in mid-air, weeping and wailing because she could not get off.

"Stop your crying," he said to her. "I will wish for all the riches in the world, only keep sitting there."

But his wife only wailed the louder, saying, "Of what use are all the riches of the world if I have to sit on this saddle? You wished me on it, now you must wish me off."

She made so much racket that the man thought his ears would burst. "All right," he cried, "I wish you may get off!"

There went his third wish! His wife was free, but the rich man gained nothing from his wishes except worry, trouble, scolding, and a dead horse. But the poor couple were contented and happy to the end of their lives.

Puss in Boots

LONG AGO there lived a miller who had three sons. When the miller died he left the mill to his eldest son, his donkey to the second son, and for the youngest son there was nothing left but the cat. Now the eldest son and the second son were happy with their share. But the third son was sad, for how could anyone make a living with only a cat?

"Alas," said the boy. "I could sell the cat's skin for a penny or make me a cap of it. But what else is a cat good for? I'll starve surely."

As the youngest son sat thus bemoaning his fate, the cat heard him. Going up to his woeful young master he said, "Good master, do not be downhearted. If you will but get me a pair of boots and a large bag with a drawstring, I shall make your living for you."

Realizing that this was no ordinary cat, but a wise and clever one, the boy did as he was bade. As soon as Puss had his boots and his bag, he hurried into the nearby wood. Putting some clover and buttercups into his bag and leaving it invitingly open, he lay down and pretended to sleep. Along hopped a foolish fat rabbit, who, smelling the green stuff in the bag, hopped in after it. Quick as a wink, Puss in Boots pulled the drawstring tight and had the rabbit in the bag.

Then he hastened to the royal palace and asked to see

the King. When he came before the ruler Puss bowed low
and said, "Sire, I have here a fine hare which has been sent
you by my lord the Marquis of Carabas." And Puss smiled
behind his whiskers, thinking of the noble, high-sounding
name he had made up for his master.

The King thanked him, for the hare was indeed a fine
one, and Puss in Boots departed.

Next day Puss went out again with his bag. This time he
baited it with grain. Again he left it open and lay down to
a pretended nap. Along came a fine fat partridge, who,
seeing the grain in the open bag, went in after it. At once
sly Puss in Boots drew the string tight and the partridge was
caught. As before, Puss in Boots went to the palace and
politely asked to see the King. When he had been admitted
to the King's presence he said, "Sire, here is a gift from the
Marquis of Carabas. He has many of these fine rare birds
upon his land."

The King was pleased with the thoughtfulness of this unknown Marquis of Carabas, and did not let on that he had
never heard the name before. Of course, no one else had
ever heard of it either, since Puss had made it up. But no
one in the King's court wanted to admit his ignorance, and
so no one ever asked who the Marquis of Carabas was.

For some time Puss in Boots continued to bring gifts to
the King, until that vain personage began to think the Marquis of Carabas must be a rich young man indeed.

One day Puss heard that the King and his lovely daughter
were going for a drive along the river. Hastening to his
young master he said, "Good master, if you will follow my
directions, I think your fortune is made."

Then he told the miller's son everything he had done,
adding that the youth must go to bathe in the river at the
exact time and the exact spot Puss in Boots should tell him.

The young man did as he was told, although he didn't see

the sense of it. As he was swimming about in the water the cat took his shabby clothes and hid them under a rock. When he heard the rumble of the King's carriage, Puss ran to the road crying, "Help! Help! The Marquis of Carabas is drowning!"

Recognizing Puss, the King stopped the carriage and ordered his servant to go and pull the Marquis out. Puss ran up to the carriage and said, "Oh, Sire, I don't know what to do. While he was swimming, my master's fine clothes were stolen."

The King sent a servant to the palace at once with orders to fetch clothes suitable for a rich nobleman. When the miller's son had donned the silken clothing, which was better than he had ever seen before, he looked so handsome that the Princess fell in love with him at sight. She begged her father to take the young man into the carriage with them.

Puss in Boots ran joyfully ahead of the carriage and was soon out of sight. When he saw some reapers in a grain field, he ran up to them and cried, "The royal coach is coming this way. When the King asks you who owns these fields, see that you answer, 'The Marquis of Carabas.' If you do not, you shall be ground up into mincemeat."

Not wanting to be ground into mincemeat, the reapers agreed. When the King approached he called out, "Who owns these fine fields?"

The reapers answered, "The Marquis of Carabas, Sire!"

Puss ran on till he came to some men who were mowing the hay in a meadow. He ran up to them and cried, "The royal coach is coming this way. When the King asks you who owns these fields, see that you answer, 'The Marquis of Carabas.' If you refuse you will be ground into mincemeat."

These people, too, obeyed the cat. So again the King was told that the land belonged to the Marquis of Carabas.

Next Puss came to a great castle in the wood. He knew it to be the castle of a terrible ogre who had the magic power to change himself into many other shapes. Going to the door, he said, "I have a message for the owner of this castle."

When he was led into the presence of the ogre, Puss said, "I have heard so much about you that I had to pay you a visit. I cannot believe that the things I hear are true. Surely you cannot change yourself into a lion!"

"Oho, can't I?" said the ogre, greatly flattered. And he promptly changed himself into a lion to prove that he could do it. At the sight of the lion Puss ran up the curtain in fright. There he clung until the ogre was himself again.

Then he came down and said, "Marvelous! Simply marvelous! You became a huge lion in a twinkling. But can you become something small? Surely it is not true that you can change into a mouse!"

"Oho, can't I?" roared the ogre, and in an instant he had become a timid little mouse.

Faster than lightning Puss pounced upon the mouse and ate him up. Then, running to the door, he saw the royal coach approaching. Holding the door wide, he called out, "Welcome to the castle of the Marquis of Carabas!"

When the King saw the rich palace the Marquis owned, and had walked through the spacious grounds, he made no objection to his daughter's marrying the young man, which she did at once. And that is how the famous Puss in Boots made his master's fortune.

Thick-Headed Jack

THERE WAS ONCE a knight who had three sons. Two of them were extremely clever, but the third was considered quite stupid. He went by the name of "Thick-headed Jack."

Now it happened that the King of that land had a daughter who was very beautiful. She was so beautiful that all the young men who came to court her were struck dumb at the mere sight of her. And if she smiled at them or asked them a question, they lost their wits completely. The Princess grew tired of this and she was determined to marry a man who knew how to give a ready answer and to think quickly. So she sent out a proclamation saying that any man in the kingdom might come and try his luck.

Both of the clever sons wished to marry the Princess, and so they spent a whole week getting ready to call on her. The eldest knew the whole Latin dictionary by heart and could recite every column of the daily newspaper for the past three years. The second brother studied law and knew about state affairs.

"I shall marry the Princess," they both declared. And they smeared their lips with sweet oil so that they wouldn't get dry and prevent a quick answer.

Their old father gave each of them a beautiful horse and his blessing. Just as they were starting off, up came the youngest brother and wanted to know where they were

going. When they said they were going to try to win the
King's daughter, Thick-headed Jack exclaimed, "Well! I
think I shall go too."

The brothers laughed scornfully and rode away.

"Father," begged Thick-headed Jack, "give me a horse.
I've a mind to win the Princess myself."

"Hold your foolish tongue," cried his father. "You shall
have no horse from me. You must not expect to do the
things your brothers do."

"Well," said Thick-headed Jack, "if I can't have a horse
I'll take my old goat." So saying, he mounted the old goat,
and went off down the road.

"Hello!" called Jack, catching up with his brothers. "See
what I found on the road." And he showed them a dead
crow.

"Blockhead," cried his brothers. "What are you going to
do with that?"

"Why, I am going to give it to the Princess, of course."

"You had better not," said his brothers, riding off at a
great speed. Jack dug his heels into the goat's side to make
him go faster and soon caught up with his brothers.

"Hippety-hop! Here I come!" he called out. "See what I
have found now. It is not everybody who could pick this up
from the turnpike road."

The brothers turned to see what he had.

"Stupid!" they cried. "That is nothing but an old wooden
shoe with the top part broken off. Are you going to give that
to the Princess?"

"Perhaps I may," said Thick-headed Jack.

The brothers laughed and rode off at a gallop until they
were a long way ahead.

"Hippety-hop! Here I come!" cried Jack, as he caught up
to his brothers for the third time. "Better and better! My,
this is splendid!"

"What have you found now?" asked the brothers.

"Oh, I can't tell you," said Jack. "It's too nice. Won't the King's daughter be pleased?"

"Dunce!" cried the brothers. "That's nothing but mud."

"Yes," agreed Jack, "but just look at the quality. It's so fine it slips right through one's fingers." Thereupon he filled his pockets with the mud.

When the brothers reached the town they had to stand in line with hundreds of other suitors. All the people of the land stood in crowds around the palace windows to see the Princess receive her beaux. As soon as one of them entered the hall where the beautiful Princess was seated, he was struck dumb with awe.

Then the King's daughter would exclaim, "Away with him," and the servants dragged each one out by the heels.

At last it came the turn of the brother who knew the Latin dictionary, but he had stood in line so long that he had forgotten every word of it. Besides, the room was as hot as an oven.

He was determined to say something, but all he could think of was, "It is dreadfully hot here."

"That's because we're roasting geese today," said the Princess, and she laughed at her own joke for the lad certainly looked as silly as any goose in a barnyard.

"Ahem! Ahem!" was all he could answer.

"He is no good," said the King's daughter. "Out with him!" And out he went by the heels. The second brother acted as stupidly as the first, and he, too, was dragged away.

Next, Thick-headed Jack came galloping straight into the room, goat and all. "Puff, it's murdering hot," he cried.

"Yes, but I am roasting geese," said the Princess.

"That's lucky for me," said Thick-headed Jack. "Will you let me roast my crow, too?"

"With pleasure," said the Princess. "Do you have anything in which to cook the crow?"

"I have indeed," said Jack. "Here is a cooking pot complete with handle." He took out the old wooden shoe and put the crow inside.

"We could have a regular meal," said the Princess, who loved to talk nonsense, "if we only had some stuffing."

"I've got some here in my pocket," said Thick-headed Jack, taking out some mud and pouring it on top of the crow.

"Now, I like that," said the Princess. "You always have an answer ready, and you aren't afraid to speak. I choose you for my husband. But, do you know that every word we have spoken is written down, and will come out in the papers tomorrow? In front of every window you see in this room there are three reporters. That old one over there is in a terrible fix, for he is deaf as a post and cannot hear a thing." She only said that to see if she could stump Jack. The reporters shook so with laughter that they dropped a shower of ink spots on the floor.

But Jack had an answer ready. "Oh, indeed?" said he. "Well, don't worry. I'll give him something to write about." With that, he took out a fistful of mud from his pocket and threw it right in the reporter's face.

"That was neatly done," said the Princess. "I could not have thought of a better answer myself."

And so it happened that Thick-headed Jack married the beautiful Princess, and when her father died several years later, Jack was made King and wore a crown.

The Elves and the Shoemaker

THERE WAS ONCE a shoemaker who worked hard and was honest, but still he could not earn enough to live on. At last, all he had in the world was gone except enough leather to make one pair of shoes. So that night he cut out the leather by candlelight and left it on his workbench ready to make up into shoes the next morning. Then, leaving all his cares to heaven, he went peacefully to sleep.

In the morning when he went to his workbench, there stood the shoes already made. The good man didn't know what to say or think of this strange event. He picked up the shoes and put them down again. He scratched his head and blinked his eyes. But there stood the shoes. He was not dreaming. He looked at the workmanship; there was not one false stitch in the whole job, and all was neat and true.

The same day a customer came in, and the shoes pleased him so much that he willingly paid a price higher than usual for them. With the money, the shoemaker bought enough leather to make two more pairs of shoes. In the evening he cut out the leather and went to bed early so that he might get up and begin his work by sunrise.

But when he got up at sunrise the work was finished. Presently buyers came who paid him handsomely for his shoes, and he bought leather enough for four more pairs. He cut out the four pairs of shoes at night, and, as before, found them finished in the morning. So it went on for some time; what was made ready in the evening was always done by daybreak, and the good shoemaker soon became thriving and prosperous in his business again.

One evening just before Christmas as the shoemaker and his wife were sitting before the fire chatting, he said to her, "I should like to sit up and watch tonight so we may see who it is that comes and does my work for me." The wife liked the idea. So they left a light burning and hid themselves behind a curtain to see what would happen, without being seen themselves.

At midnight two little elves came in and sat themselves upon the shoemaker's bench. They had neither coats to their backs nor shoes to their feet but were as naked as peeled onions. They took up the work that was cut out and began turning and stitching and rapping and tapping at such a rate that the shoemaker watched in amazement. On they worked until the job was finished, and the shoes stood ready upon the table. Then the little elves bustled away as quickly and as silently as they had come.

The next day the wife said to the shoemaker, "These little men have made us rich, and we ought to show our thanks. I am quite upset to see them running about with not a stitch on their backs to keep them warm. I'll tell you what. I will make each of them a shirt, a coat, waistcoat, and a pair of pantaloons into the bargain. You make each of them a little pair of shoes."

This thought pleased the good shoemaker very much, and he set to work. One evening, when all the things were ready, he laid the clothes on the worktable. Then the shoemaker and his wife hid themselves in order to watch what the little creatures would do.

About midnight the elves came in and were going to sit down to their work as usual. When they saw the clothes

lying there for them, they laughed and clapped their hands.
They dressed themselves in the twinkling of an eye, and
danced and capered and sprang about as merry as sunbeams.
At last they danced out of the door and the shoemaker saw
them no more, but from that time forward everything went
well for him as long as he lived.

Aladdin and the Wonderful Lamp

IN FAR EASTERN LANDS there was once a magician who, through his magic books, learned about a wonderful lamp. He alone knew where to find this lamp, but he could not get it by himself, for the lamp would have no magic power until it left the hand of its finder and was touched by another. So the magician sought some stupid person to get the lamp for him.

Now it happened that the magician met a poor boy named Aladdin. Aladdin's father had just died and his mother was having a hard time of it, for she had no relatives of her own to look after her and she did not know where her husband's family lived. The wicked magician rubbed his hands with glee when he heard all this, for he thought that Aladdin would be just the one to help him get the lamp.

So he bought a basket of fruit as a present and went to Aladdin saying, "I am your long lost uncle, the brother of your dear dead father. Ah, I would have known you anywhere, for you look so much like him. Take this fruit to your mother and ask her if I am welcome in her house."

Aladdin raced home and told his mother the news. Of course she was overjoyed to find someone to help her, and she prepared the best meal possible and bade the false uncle welcome.

Next day the false uncle bought new clothes for Aladdin

and took him all over town, telling him to look carefully and choose the sort of trade he would like to follow, and promising to set him up in any business he selected. Aladdin now trusted the man completely and was ready to do anything he asked.

On the second day the magician took Aladdin on a long walk outside the city gates, through beautiful gardens and up into the hills—farther than Aladdin had ever been before. At length they came to a fountain springing up between two hills.

"We shall go no farther," said the false uncle. "Gather sticks for a fire so that we may cook our dinner."

Aladdin did as he was told, but when the fire was blazing, instead of cooking the dinner the magician tossed a magic powder into the flames and mumbled some strange words. Immediately the ground shook beneath their feet. The fire vanished in a great cloud of hissing smoke and in its place was a square flat stone with a brass ring in the middle.

Aladdin's teeth were chattering with terror, and he would have run away but the magician caught him by the ear and cuffed him soundly.

"Stay here," he hissed. "The greatest treasure in the world lies beneath that stone, and you try to run away."

At the word *treasure,* Aladdin forgot his fears and listened to what the magician was saying.

"Place this ring on your finger," ordered the magician. "Then lift the stone."

Aladdin placed the ring on his finger. Then he took hold of the stone to lift it, and it came up easily, revealing a narrow, winding stone staircase.

"Descend the stairs," commanded the magician. "But take care lest your clothes touch the walls, for if they do so you will die. At the end of the passageway you will find a lighted lamp. Pour out the oil and bring the lamp to me."

Aladdin descended the stairs and found himself in a narrow passageway bordered with fruit trees. The fruit gleamed so brightly that Aladdin plucked some and filled his pockets. He found the lamp and returned with it to the staircase.

The wicked magician was waiting with outstretched hands at the top of the stairs.

"The lamp, the lamp!" he cried. "Give it to me."

But Aladdin was too clever to give up the lamp until he was safely out of the pit.

"You shall have it when I am ready to give it to you," the boy answered.

At this the magician flew into a fit of temper and slammed the flat stone back in place, leaving Aladdin in blackness. The poor youth was afraid to move an inch for fear his garments would touch the walls of the cave and bring him instant death. He crouched on the steps for what seemed an endless time. At last, he clasped his hands in prayer, and in so doing he rubbed the magic ring which the magician had placed on his finger.

Instantly a hissing cloud of smoke rose before him and in its midst was a genie who bowed low, saying, "Master of the Ring, I am your slave. Command and I obey."

Scarcely daring to believe his good fortune, Aladdin said, "Bring me up again into the sunlight."

The words were no sooner spoken than he found himself above ground and the sun shining brightly. He hastened home and told his mother all that had happened. When he drew forth the fruit he had picked in the passageway, he discovered that it was not fruit, but jewels.

"They are of no use to us," said his mother sadly, "for if we tried to sell such valuables we would be hanged for thieves."

"We can at least sell the lamp," said Aladdin. "No one

would suspect us of stealing such a dirty old thing."

"Let me have it," said his mother, and she took it in her hands and began to polish it with her apron, thinking that a clean lamp would bring a higher price.

Instantly a genie appeared in a cloud of smoke. The poor woman nearly fainted with fright, and would have dropped the lamp, but Aladdin caught it and said, "Bring us food."

The smoke cleared away, leaving a table richly spread with silver bowls and dishes, all filled with the most tempting and luscious food. Aladdin helped his mother to her feet, and they sat down to the feast.

For some time afterward they lived well on the money gained by selling the silver dishes, one at a time. When these were all gone, Aladdin summoned the genie again, and thus they were never in need of anything.

Now it chanced one day that Aladdin caught a glimpse of the daughter of the Emperor while the Princess was on her way to the river with her ladies-in-waiting. The beauty of the Princess was so dazzling that Aladdin fell in love with her at sight and longed to have her for his wife. So, according to the custom of the country, he told his mother to go to the Emperor and ask for the Princess as his bride.

The good woman was filled with horror, for it was an unheard-of thing that the son of a poor widow should marry a Princess. But Aladdin begged her to go and take the jewels from the magic cave as a gift, and at last she agreed.

At first the Emperor would not even listen to her request, but when she unfolded her scarf and showed him the jewels, his eyes lighted greedily.

"Ah, my good woman," he said. "If your son truly wants to marry my daughter he will send me forty golden baskets each heaped to the brim with precious jewels. Do this, and then I will listen to what you have to say."

So the woman went home and told Aladdin, who immediately summoned the genie and demanded the forty golden baskets of jewels. Then once more Aladdin's mother went to the Emperor and asked that her son be allowed to marry the beautiful Princess.

The Emperor did not intend to let such a son-in-law escape, and he agreed immediately that the wedding should take place. Aladdin, however, said that he must wait until he had built a palace worthy of his bride, and the Emperor gave him the land right next to his own estate. Of course, Aladdin then summoned the genie of the lamp. Building a palace was no more difficult for the genie than providing a meal. Before the nightingales in the palace garden could finish one trill there appeared a domed palace with windows of rubies and diamonds. It was complete to the smallest detail, and there was even a roast pig in the oven.

The wedding was performed without delay, and Aladdin took his beautiful bride home to their new castle. He was so noble and kind that she loved him dearly. Indeed, in a short time everyone in the whole country was praising the handsome young Prince Aladdin.

But alas for happiness! Far, far across the sea in deepest Africa the wicked magician heard of Aladdin's success and knew that only the wonderful lamp could have given him such wealth and power. His evil heart was wild with rage, and he determined to bring about Aladdin's ruin. Forthwith he set out and traveled night and day until he came to the town where Aladdin lived. Disguising himself as a ragged merchant, he went about the streets with a basket of shiny new lamps, crying out:

"New lamps for old; new lamps for old.
Who will trade me new lamps for old?"

Now Aladdin was out hunting at the time, but his wife

heard the lamp merchant and thought it would be amusing to see if the old fellow really would do such a silly thing as trade a new lamp for an old one. She looked all over the palace for the oldest lamp she could find, and of course chose the magic lamp which Aladdin had hidden in a corner without saying anything to her about it. No sooner did the old magician have the magic lamp in his hands than he whisked out of sight. Once he was away from the crowds, he rubbed the lamp, and ordered the genie to transport the palace, with the Princess in it, across the sea to deepest Africa.

When the Emperor discovered that his daughter had vanished, he ordered Aladdin to be brought before him and threatened to cut off Aladdin's head if he did not restore the Princess and the palace immediately. Aladdin, half-crazed with grief, begged for time in which to accomplish this task, and the Emperor granted him forty days and forty nights in which to find the Princess.

Aladdin then went to a secret place, rubbed the magic ring, and when the genie appeared, Aladdin commanded him to restore the Princess and the palace.

"That I cannot do," said the genie. "Only the Slave of the Lamp can undo what has been done."

"Then take me to my Princess, wherever she may be," ordered Aladdin, and as quick as breath he found himself in his own palace beside his sleeping bride. She awakened with a start and clasped him in her arms for joy. But her joy turned to tears as she told him of the wicked magician.

"Do not fear," Aladdin told her. "Put this powder in his wine when he joins you at supper, drink none yourself, and leave all else to me."

Then Aladdin hid himself behind a curtain, and the Princess did as he had commanded her.

The magician came and drained the poisoned wine to the

last drop. Instantly he fell to the floor, lifeless. Aladdin sprang from his hiding place and seized the lamp which the magician had hidden in his shirt. Rubbing it hastily, Aladdin ordered the genie to take the palace and everyone in it back where they had come from. As swiftly and gently as the whispering wind, the order was accomplished.

The Emperor welcomed his daughter and Aladdin with joyous feasting that lasted ten days and ten nights. And when the years passed and the Emperor grew old, Aladdin reigned and the whole land prospered and was happy.

The Three Sillies

ONCE THERE LIVED a peasant whose fields were quite a long way from his house, and every noon his daughter would bring his lunch to him in a little basket. One day the girl grew tired before she had gone half the distance, and so she sat down under a tree to rest. Soon she began to daydream.

"Ah," she thought, "some day I shall be married and I shall have a baby boy and name him Stoyan." But no sooner had she thought this than she imagined that the child would die.

"Oy, O!" she cried. "My poor dead son." And she wept.

The girl was gone so long that her mother came to look for her. The good woman was greatly astonished to find the girl sitting under the tree and weeping as if her heart would break.

"Daughter, daughter," cried the woman. "What ails you?"

"Boo-hoo-hoo," sobbed the girl. "If I should have a son and he should die! Oy, O! My poor dead little Stoyan."

On hearing this the woman burst into tears also and cried out, "Oh, my poor dead grandson. Oh, the pity of it."

And the two of them sat and cried all afternoon.

By and by the peasant came home, his stomach empty and his temper none too soft. When he found his wife and daughter weeping and wailing and learned the cause of their woes, he was about to beat them black and blue. But instead he said, "You shall never see me again unless I have found three fools who are sillier than you."

And so saying, he took his lunch and set out on his travels.

By and by he came to a village where some people were building a house. But they had forgotten to put any windows in it, and so they were carrying huge chests full of sunshine into the house to make it bright and cheery. Of course when they opened the chests there was no sunshine in them, and so they were weeping and wailing and making a great fuss.

"How much money will you give me if I help you?" asked the peasant.

"Whatever you wish," said the silly people.

So the peasant took a saw and cut out some openings for windows, and the silly people clapped their hands in wonder at his cleverness and filled his pockets with gold and silver.

In a short while he met a man who had tied his trousers to a bush and was climbing a tree beside them.

"Whatever are you doing?" asked the peasant.

"Getting into my trousers," said the man, "and having a terrible time of it. Every time I jump down into them, the wind blows them aside. I either get the left leg where the right one goes, or the right leg where the left one goes, or miss them both altogether."

So the peasant showed the silly man how to lean up against the tree and pull his trousers on one leg at a time, and once again the peasant was rewarded with silver and gold.

On he went and in good time he saw two women sitting in a dooryard with a fat pig running near them.

"Ah, good day," said the peasant. "How lucky I am to find you at home. I've come to take your pig to a wedding, for his brother is getting married."

"Oh, oh," squealed the silly women in great delight. And they scurried about to get the little pig dressed up in great style for the occasion.

"Let's use the silk shawl," said one.

"Pin on this lace collar," said the other.

"Use my gold necklace."

"Take my silver earrings."

And they dressed the pig in all their finery and gave it to the peasant without asking another question.

Off the peasant went with the pig under his arm and never stopped until he was back in his own house. His wife and daughter met him, trembling in their boots for fear of getting a beating. But the peasant only handed them the pig and told them to cook it at once and be quick about it.

So instead of getting a beating, they all got roast pig for supper. And if you stop by their house I'm sure they will give you a bite.

Tom Thumb

MANY, MANY YEARS AGO the great magician Merlin, dressed as a beggar, stopped at a peasant's cottage one evening. He was given a hearty welcome and the wife brought out a pitcher of milk and some fresh bread for him.

Although everything was neat and comfortable about the cottage, the peasant and his wife seemed sad. Merlin asked what the trouble was and learned that the couple were grieving because they had no children.

"If we only had a son," the woman said. "Even if he were no larger than my husband's thumb, I would be satisfied."

The idea of a boy no larger than a man's thumb pleased Merlin. Being a magician, he knew how to manage so that in good time a child, no larger than the peasant's thumb, was born to the couple.

The Fairy Queen heard of the wee chap and came to see him. She said she would be his godmother and gave him the name of Tom Thumb. Then she sent for her fairies to come and dress the tiny boy. They made him a hat of an oak leaf, a shirt of spider's web, a jacket of thistledown. His trousers were made of feathers, his stockings of apple peeling, and his shoes were made of mouse skin with the fur inside.

As time went on, Tom did not grow a quarter of an inch

in size, but he became cunning and full of tricks. One time when he was playing a game of cherry stones with some playmates, he lost all his stones in the game. Then he slyly stole into the bag of one of the other boys and was just climbing out with his pockets full of stones when one of the boys saw him.

"Ah ha, Tom! That is where you get your cherry stones," he said. "I'll fix you this time!" And he pulled the string of the bag around Tom and shook it so that Tom was quite bruised.

One morning soon after this, Tom's mother was making a pudding. Tom wanted to see just how it was made and when his mother wasn't looking he climbed upon the edge of the bowl. Down he slipped and fell into the batter. He tried to call out, but the batter got in his mouth and he could not say a word. When his mother put the pudding on to boil, Tom jumped so hard that his mother thought the pudding was bewitched and threw it out the window.

A tinker was passing by. He saw the fine pudding and picked it up. He was about to put it in his knapsack, when Tom called out loudly. The tinker was so frightened that he threw the pudding over the fence and went off. Tom managed to scramble out of the batter and hurried home as fast as he could. His mother put him in a teacup of soapsuds and gave him a good scrubbing, for he was covered with pudding dough.

A few days later Tom's mother took him with her when she went to milk the cow. The wind was blowing and she feared that Tom might be blown away, so she fastened him to a thistle with a piece of thread. The cow, seeing Tom's oak-leaf hat, thought it was something good to eat, and took Tom and the thistle in one bite. Tom was afraid of the cow's great teeth, and he called out, "Mother! Mother!"

"Where are you, Tom?" his mother called.

"I'm here in the cow's mouth," Tom answered.

Tom's mother did not know what to do, but the cow, hearing a queer noise in her throat, let Tom drop. Tom's mother caught him in her apron and took him home.

Another time, Tom's father made him a whip of straw to help him drive the cattle. One day when Tom was taking the cattle to pasture, he stumbled and fell. A raven saw him and picked him up. He carried Tom far up in the air and when they were out at sea, the raven let the boy drop. A fish came along and swallowed Tom, but the fish was soon caught and brought to the kitchen of the palace.

When the cook cut open the fish, out stepped Tom Thumb. The cook was speechless with amazement, but after she'd got her senses again, she took the wee lad to the King's court, where Tom soon became a favorite.

One day the King asked Tom about his parents. On hearing that Tom's father and mother were poor, the King asked him how he would like to go home for a visit and take them some money. Tom was overjoyed with this idea. The King took the boy to his treasury and told him to take as much money as he could carry. Tom took his purse made of a water bubble and put in it a silver three-penny piece.

This was a heavy load, but he managed to take it on his back, and started for home. All day and all night and all the next day he traveled. He was terribly tired when he reached home, and his mother hugged and kissed him and put him straight to bed.

He rested at home for several days, and then he said he must return to the court, for the King wanted him. His parents grieved to see him go, but go he must. His mother made a tiny umbrella, and with Tom holding tightly to the handle, she blew him toward the palace. Just as Tom was floating across the yard the cook was crossing it with a bowl of porridge for the King. Down, down came Tom, and landed right in the center of the porridge with a great splash. The cook was splattered from head to toe with the sticky stuff.

She was angry and told the King that Tom had splattered her on purpose. As the King was busy with other affairs, the cook put Tom into a wire mousetrap and kept him imprisoned there. A whole week passed before the King asked again for Tom. He pardoned Tom for throwing the porridge about, and once more took him into favor. The King made Tom a knight and from that time on he was known as Sir Thomas Thumb.

As Tom's clothes had suffered from the pudding batter, the insides of the fish, and the porridge, the King ordered a new suit made for Tom. The fairy tailors came to his aid and made him a shirt of butterflies' wings and boots of chicken leather. Then he was given a darning needle to use as a sword, and a nimble gray mouse for a steed.

It was quite a sight to see Tom in his new clothes, mounted on his steed, as he went riding with the members of the court.

One day as they were riding past a farmhouse, a cat ran out, and before anyone could stop her, she grabbed the mouse. Tom fought bravely, but the cat would not give up her prey and Tom was scratched sorely in the struggle.

The Queen of Fairyland came by just then and took Tom back to Fairyland for a visit. There he stayed for many years.

When he returned to the King's palace, the King ordered a tiny gold chair made, so that he could sit at the royal table. He also gave Tom a tiny coach drawn by six small mice. And Tom lived happily for many years and was known far and wide for his bravery and his cunning.

The Spindle, the Shuttle, and the Needle

THERE WAS ONCE a little girl who lived with her godmother in a small cottage at the far end of a village. They earned their living by spinning, weaving, and sewing, and the child grew up to be very industrious. When the girl was about fifteen, her godmother died and left her the cottage, the spindle, the shuttle, and the needle.

The girl lived alone in the cottage, and everything she did turned out well. Whenever she wove a piece of cloth, she immediately found a purchaser, who paid her so well that she had plenty for herself and could always spare a little for others who were poorer.

About this time, the King's son was looking for a bride, but he was not allowed to marry a poor wife, and he did not want a rich one. So he said, "My bride must be at once both the richest and the poorest."

When the Prince arrived at the village where the girl lived, he asked the people to name the richest and poorest maidens in the place. They named the richest, and then told him that the poorest was the young maiden who lived in the cottage at the end of the village.

The young Prince first went to the rich maiden, and found her beautifully dressed sitting before her door with her hands folded in her lap. The Prince bowed politely but said not a word, and rode to the house of the poor maiden.

She was not seated idly at the door, but was in her little room working busily. The Prince alighted from his horse and peeped into the neat cottage. At that moment a ray of sunshine sparkled through the window, lighting up every-thing inside. The Prince saw the maiden spinning at her wheel.

Presently she glanced up and, seeing a noble-looking gentleman peering at her through the window, she blushed, cast down her eyes, and continued her spinning until the Prince rode away. Then she rose and opened the window, saying to herself, "How very warm the sun is today," not realizing that it was her own blushes, not the sun, that made her seem warm.

She watched the handsome stranger until he was quite out of sight, and then returned to her spinning wheel.

However, her thoughts were now on the handsome Prince, although she did not know who he was. Strange ideas came into her head, and she began to sing some curious words which her dear godmother had taught her:

> "Spindle, spindle, out with you,
> Bring me home a lover true."

To her surprise the spindle leaped from her hands and rushed out of the house. She followed it to the door and stood looking after it with wondering eyes, for it was running and dancing merrily across the field, trailing a golden thread behind it. Then she took up her shuttle, seated herself, and began weaving. The spindle, meanwhile, kept on its way, and just as the thread came to an end, it overtook the Prince.

"What do I see?" he cried. "The thread behind this spindle will lead me to good fortune, no doubt." So he turned his horse and followed the trail of the golden thread.

The maiden, who still worked on, thought of another rhyme taught to her by the old woman. So she sang:

> "Shuttle, shuttle, weave, I pray,
> A carpet for my lover gay."

Instantly, the shuttle slipped from her hand and ran to the door, but on the doorsill it stopped and began to weave the most beautiful carpet ever seen.

Then the maiden sang:

> "Needle, needle, sharp and fine,
> Fit the house for lover mine."

As soon as she said this the needle sprang from her hand and flew about the room as quick as lightning. The table and benches were quickly covered with green cloth, the chairs with velvet, and curtains were hung at the window.

The needle had scarcely finished the last stitch when the maiden saw through the window the plume on the Prince's hat. He had followed the golden thread until it reached her cottage. He alighted from his horse and stepped in on the beautiful carpet. When he entered, he saw the maiden, who, even in her homely dress, was as lovely as a wild rose.

"You are exactly what I have been looking for," he said. "Both the poorest and the richest maiden in the world. Will you come with me and be my bride?"

She said nothing but smiled shyly and held out her hand. The Prince took it and, giving her a kiss, led her out of the cottage and seated her behind him on his horse. He took her to his father's castle, where the wedding was celebrated with great feasting and merrymaking.

The spindle, the shuttle, and the needle were placed in the treasure-chamber of the palace, and the girl cherished them as long as she lived.

How the Sea Became Salt

IN A SMALL VILLAGE far over the sea there once lived two brothers. One was rich, but the other was very poor. One Christmas Eve the poor brother found he had nothing at all in the house to eat, neither crust nor crumbs. He went to the rich brother and begged for something, even a little flour.

The rich brother was selfish as well as rich, and he did not care to be bothered with the poor brother. However, he said, "There is a side of fat bacon in the smokehouse you may have, but know this. It is the last thing you shall get from me. Never come here again to ask for anything."

The poor brother took the bacon, thanked his brother, and set out for home. He was going along the path in the forest when a little old man stepped out in front of him.

"Good evening," said the poor brother.

"Good evening to you," the little old man said. "Where are you going with that bacon?"

"I am on my way home to take it to my wife. We have nothing to eat in the house, and it is Christmas Eve."

"If you will go down this path a little way," the old man directed him, "you will find an enchanter's palace. Go inside, and you will be surrounded by the enchanter's imps. They will want to buy the bacon from you, for there is nothing enchanter's imps like better than fat bacon. But do not sell it to them for money. Ask for the old mill that stands behind the door in exchange for the meat. Bring the mill back to me and I will show you how to use it."

The poor brother went on and came to the castle. On entering it, he was surrounded by the imps clamoring for the bacon. They tried to make all sorts of bargains with him, but he insisted on having the old mill behind the door. Finally the imps gave him the mill and ran off with the meat.

The poor brother took the mill under his arm and went back to the little old man, who showed him how the mill was to be used. The brother had but to say, "Grind, mill, grind," and name what he wanted.

But to make the mill stop after he had used it, it had to be set in a certain position.

The poor man thanked the stranger for his help and went home. It was dark before he reached there, and his wife was worrying about what might have happened to him.

"I have been waiting all day," the wife said, "and there is neither bread nor bone in the whole house. I am so hungry that I am almost dead."

"Tell your hunger good-bye," the man said, "for see what I have brought you."

He put the mill on the table and said, "Grind, mill, grind." Asking for a holiday supper, he turned the handle. Immediately a cloth was spread and all sorts of good dishes were set out on the table. The wife looked on with awe.

"Where did you get such a mill?" she asked.

"Do not bother your head about it," was the only answer he would give.

How they enjoyed their supper! It had been a long time since they had had so many good things to eat.

Three days later the poor brother gave a party to which he invited all his friends and his rich brother as well.

"Where did you get all this wealth so suddenly?" the rich brother asked. "Only Christmas Eve you were begging for something to eat, and now you entertain like a duke."

"I found it behind the door," the poor brother answered, for he did not intend to tell his secret.

One night, however, he could hold his tongue no longer, and he told his brother about the mill.

From that time on, the rich brother tried in every way to get possession of the mill. At last the poor brother promised that if he could keep the mill until harvest time, he would then sell it to his rich brother for three hundred pounds.

The poor brother made good use of the mill that summer. He tried to think of everything he would possibly want for many years to come. When harvest time came, he gave the mill to his brother and told him what to say to start it grinding. But he did not tell him how to stop the mill, and his brother was so anxious to get the treasure that he did not stop to ask.

The morning after the rich man got the mill, he sent his wife and servants to the field, saying he would stay home himself and get the dinner. When dinnertime came, he set the mill upon the table and said, "Grind, grind, serve up herrings and milk soup."

The mill at once began to grind out herrings and milk soup. The rich man filled enough bowls for dinner and then said, "You can stop now."

But the mill did not stop. The man filled all the pots and pans, but the mill still went on. Herrings and milk soup, herrings and milk soup all over the place.

"Whoa!" called the man. "Halt! Stop! Quit!" But the mill kept on grinding out the herrings and milk soup. They ran down on the floor; they flooded the room. The man opened the door, and the herrings and milk soup ran out into the hall. The rich man flopped and floundered through the sticky stuff and opened the front door and the milk soup and herrings ran out into the garden.

Meanwhile his wife, at work in the fields, wondered why her husband had not called her to dinner. Perhaps he was having trouble preparing the meal.

"Let us go home," she said to the reapers. "My husband must be finding it difficult to get the dinner."

So the wife and the reapers started for home. As they came to the garden, they saw the river of milk soup and herrings rushing toward them. In the midst of it was the man, floundering about and holding the mill over his head.

"Take care that this dinner does not drown you," he called to the workers, and then he hurried on his way to the house of his poor brother.

"Take it back," he begged. "Stop it or the whole village will be flooded with milk soup and herrings."

The poor brother took the mill and stopped it, but he charged three hundred pounds for doing so. The only thing the rich brother could do was to pay the sum, for he was at the mercy of his brother.

With this money and what he had saved, the poor brother now built a beautiful house. It stood on the seashore and since the walls were covered with gold, it could be seen for many miles out at sea. The house and its owner became known far and wide, and people from all over the world came to see it.

Among those who came to this wonderful house was a sea captain. He had heard about the magic mill and wished to see it. He asked if the mill could grind out salt and was told that it certainly could.

"How fine it would be if I had that mill," the captain thought. "I would no longer have to sail the seas, but could stay in port and still have a ship always loaded with cargo. I could just ask the mill to grind salt and my ship would be filled. How much money I could make!"

The sea captain pleaded and begged to buy the mill. At

first the brother refused, but at last he consented to sell it for a great sum of money. As soon as the captain had the mill in his possession, he hurried away for fear the owner would change his mind and demand the return of the mill. The captain left without waiting to find out how to stop the mill.

As soon as he was back on his ship, he set down the mill and said, "Grind, mill, grind. Fill my ship with salt." And the mill began to grind salt.

Soon the hold of the ship was filled with salt and piles of it stood on the deck. The ship began to creak and groan under the weight.

"Stop! Stop!" bellowed the captain. But the mill went on grinding. It ground and it ground and it ground salt and still more salt. Finally the ship broke down under the weight and sank to the bottom of the sea, but the mill still went on grinding. To this very day the mill lies at the bottom of the sea grinding salt.

And that is how the sea became salt.

The Nose

A LONG TIME AGO three poor soldiers, after having fought hard in the wars, set out on their road toward home begging their way as they went.

One evening when they reached a deep and gloomy wood, darkness came upon them, and they found that they must spend the night there. They agreed that two of them should sleep, while a third kept guard so that no wild beasts could harm them. When the guard grew tired, he was to awaken one of the others and take his turn at sleeping.

The two who were to rest first lay down and fell fast asleep, while the third built a fire and sat down to keep watch. He had not waited long before a little man in a red jacket appeared.

"Who's there?" the little man asked.

"A friend," said the soldier.

"What sort of a friend?"

"A poor broken-down soldier," said the other, "with his two comrades who have nothing left to live on. Come, sit down and warm yourself."

"Thank you for your courtesy," said the little man. "Since kindness should never go unrewarded, take this and show it to your comrades in the morning."

He took an old cloak from his pocket and gave it to the soldier, telling him that whoever wore it would get whatever he wished. Then the little man vanished.

The second soldier's turn to watch soon came, and the first went to sleep. Before long the little man in the red jacket appeared again. The second soldier was as friendly as his comrade had been, and the little man gave him a purse, which he told him would always be full of gold.

Then the third soldier's turn to watch came, and he also had the little man for his guest. He received a wonderful horn that drew crowds whenever it was played and made everyone do what the blower commanded.

In the morning each soldier told his story and showed his treasure. As they were old friends, they agreed to travel together to see the world. They spent their time very happily, until at last they began to tire of this roving life and thought they would like to have a home of their own. So the first soldier put on his cloak and wished for a fine castle. In a moment it stood before their eyes with fine gardens and green lawns spread around it. Out of the gate came a fine coach with three dapple-gray horses to meet the three soldiers and take them to their new home.

All went very well for a time. But it would not do to stay at home always, so they gathered all their rich clothes and servants, ordered their coach, and set out on a journey to see a neighboring King. Now this King had an only daughter, and as he took the three soldiers for king's sons, he gave them a royal welcome.

One day, as the second soldier was walking with the Princess, she saw his wonderful purse. She asked him what it was, and he was foolish enough to tell her. But indeed, it did not make much difference, for she had magic powers of her own and knew all about it anyway. Now this Princess was very cunning and artful, so she set to work and made a purse so like the soldier's that no one would know one from the other. Then she asked him to come to see her, and while he was there she gave him some wine that she had drugged.

Soon he fell asleep. The Princess took away the wonderful purse, leaving the one she had made in its place.

The next morning the soldiers started for home. Soon after they reached their castle, they wanted some money and went to their purse for it. They found money in it, but when they had emptied it, none came to take its place. The trick was soon discovered, and the second soldier told his friends where he had been and that he had told the story of the wonderful purse to the Princess. The soldiers knew at once that she had betrayed him.

"Alas!" he cried. "Whatever shall we do?"

"Oh," said the first soldier, "let no gray hairs grow for this mishap. I will soon get the purse back."

He threw his magic cloak across his shoulders and wished himself in the Princess's chamber. There he found her sitting alone, counting the gold that fell around her in a shower from the purse. The soldier accidentally dropped his cloak and the Princess saw him.

"Thieves! Thieves!" she cried loudly. The whole court came running and tried to seize him. The poor soldier forgot all about his cloak, ran to the window, opened it, and jumped out. When the Princess saw that he had left his cloak behind, she was happy, for she knew its worth.

The poor soldier made his way home on foot in a very downcast mood, but the third soldier told him not to worry, and took his horn and blew a merry tune. At the first blast, a thousand men thronged about him. At the soldier's command they set out to make war against the Princess. The King's palace was besieged, and the King was told that he must make his daughter give up the purse and cloak, or not one stone of the castle would be left standing.

The King went into his daughter's chamber and talked with her, but she said, "First let me see if I cannot beat them in some other way." Then dressing herself as a poor girl with a basket on her arm, she set out by night with her maid, and went into the enemy's camp to sell trinkets.

In the morning she rambled about, singing ballads so beautifully that all the tents were left empty, and the soldiers thought of nothing but her singing. Among those who left their tents was the soldier to whom the horn belonged. As soon as she saw him, she winked to her maid who slipped slyly through the crowd, went into his tent, and stole the horn away. This done, the maidens both got safely back to the palace, the besieging army went away, and the three wonderful gifts were all left in the hands of the Princess.

The poor soldiers were now as penniless and forlorn as when the little man with the red jacket had found them in the wood.

"Comrades," said the soldier who had owned the purse, "we had better part; we cannot live together. Let each earn his bread as well as he can." So he turned to the right, and the other two went to the left, for the two would rather travel together. The lone soldier wandered along until he came to a wood—the same wood where they had met the little man. He walked on until evening came. Then he sat down beneath a tree, and soon fell asleep.

Morning dawned, and he was delighted, on opening his eyes, to see that the tree under which he lay was laden with the most beautiful apples. He was hungry, so he plucked and ate first one, then another, then a third apple.

Suddenly his nose began to itch furiously. When he put up his hand to scratch it, he discovered that his nose had grown down to his chin. In a minute it reached his breast. It did not stop there, but continued to grow and grow.

"Mercy on us!" he thought. "When will it stop growing?" And well might he ask, for by this time it had reached the ground. On it went over the grass, across the brook, around the bushes, between the trees, stretching to an enormous length all through the wood.

Meantime, his comrades journeyed on. Suddenly one of them stumbled against something.

"What can that be?" asked the other. They looked carefully and could think of nothing that it was like but a nose.

"We will follow it and find its owner," they said. So they traced the queer thing till at last they found their poor comrade lying stretched under the apple tree.

What was to be done? They tried to carry him, but in vain. They caught a donkey that was passing by and raised him upon his back, but the beast tired of carrying such a load.

Then suddenly the little man in the red jacket appeared.

"Why, how now, friend?" he said, laughing. "I must find a cure for you, I see." He told the soldiers to bring their comrade a pear from the tree that grew close by. As soon as the soldier had eaten of it, his nose became its proper size.

"I will do something more for you," said the little man. "Take some of the magic fruit with you. Go to the Princess and get her to eat some of your apples. Her nose will grow twenty times as long as yours did; then look sharp, and you will get what you want of her."

They thanked their old friend for his kindness, and it was agreed that the poor soldier who had already tried the power of the apples should go to the Princess. He dressed himself as a gardener's boy, went to the King's palace, and said he had apples to sell such as never had been seen before. Everyone who saw the fruit was delighted and wanted to taste it, but he said the apples were only for the Princess. She sent her maid to buy his stock.

The apples were so tempting that she began eating at once. She had eaten three when she began to wonder what ailed her nose. It grew and grew, down to the ground, out of the window, and over the garden wall, and nobody knows how far.

The King announced to all his kingdom that whoever

could heal her of this dreadful disease should be richly rewarded. Many tried, but the Princess got no relief. Then the
soldier dressed himself as a doctor, and said he could cure
her.

He chopped up some of the apple, and to punish her, gave
her a dose, saying he would call the next day. Instead of being shorter, the nose was longer than ever. The Princess was
in a dreadful fright. The doctor chopped up a little of the
pear and gave it to her, saying he was sure that would do
good, and he would call again the next day. Next day the
nose was, to be sure, a little smaller, but it was still bigger
than it had been when the doctor began to meddle with it.

The doctor thought to himself, "I must frighten this cunning Princess a little more." So he gave her another dose of
the apple and said he would call on the morrow. The next
morning came, and the nose was ten times as bad as before.

"My good lady," said the doctor, "something works
against my medicine. I know what it is. You have stolen
goods about you, I am sure, and if you do not give them
back, I can do nothing for you."

The Princess denied that she had anything of the kind.

"Very well," said the doctor, "you may do as you please,
but I am sure I am right."

Then he went to the King, and told him exactly how the
matter stood.

"Daughter," the King said, "send back the cloak, the
purse, and the horn that you stole from their owners."

The Princess ordered her maid to fetch all three things,
and she gave them to the doctor, begging him to return them.
The moment he had them safe, he gave the Princess a whole
pear to eat, and the nose became normal size.

As for the doctor, he put on the cloak, wished the King
and his court a good day, and was soon with his two friends,
who ever after lived happily in their palace.

The Sleeping Beauty

LONG AND LONG AGO, in the olden days when things were still to be had by wishing for them, a King and a Queen wished that they might have a beautiful baby daughter. When the child was born the King was so overjoyed that he ordered a great feast to be prepared, and he invited the seven fairies of the kingdom to come to the baby's christening.

The seven fairies came, but with them was another fairy— quite an old one—whom the King had not invited. She had not been heard from for fifty years, and the King had forgotten all about her ever having lived in his kingdom.

The old fairy was quite angry at having been left out, and she mumbled and grumbled and acted so rude that the King began to be worried. It was the custom in those days for the guests at a christening to give presents to the child, and the King feared that perhaps the old fairy would give something evil.

The King was not the only one to think thus. The youngest fairy suspected it also, and she determined to give her gift last so that she might undo the old fairy's evil wish if it were at all possible. So with this in mind, she hid behind the curtain and waited till all the other fairies had spoken their wishes for the newborn child.

The fairies came up one by one to the crib, touched the tiny Princess with their wands and bestowed their gifts.

"She shall be the most beautiful person in all the world," said the first.

"She shall have the disposition of an angel," said the second.

"She shall have the grace of a fairy," said the third.

"She shall dance like a will-o'-the-wisp," said the fourth.

"She shall sing like a bird," said the fifth.

"She shall be able to play any instrument," said the sixth.

Then the old fairy stepped forward. "When she is sixteen years old, she shall prick her finger on a spindle and shall die from it," she said with a look of evil triumph.

Everyone gasped in dismay. But the seventh and youngest fairy came out from behind the curtains and said, "I cannot undo entirely what the last fairy has done. But I can grant that the girl shall not die but shall sleep for a hundred years."

The King thanked the youngest fairy, but to be on the safe side he immediately sent out a decree that all the spindles in the land should be burned. The King thought that now his child would be safe.

All went well for many years. The little girl grew more beautiful every day. She was so kind and thoughtful that everyone loved her dearly, and she sang and danced as no one else in the kingdom had ever done.

About the time of the Princess's sixteenth birthday, the King and Queen were extremely busy with affairs of state, and left the Princess to amuse herself. She became restless and decided to explore the whole castle from the deepest dungeon to the highest tower.

Far up in a tower she saw a door that she had never seen before. Of course, she opened it, and inside there sat a little old woman spinning. It was the old fairy, in disguise.

"What are you doing?" the Princess asked, for she had never before seen anyone spin.

The woman held out her spindle and invited the girl to sit down and spin.

The Princess was eager to try this new occupation and she held out her hand to take the spindle. No sooner had she touched it than she fell on the couch as if dead. But she was not dead. She was asleep.

Then all over the castle people began to nod and doze. The King began to snore right in the middle of a conference, and all the statesmen put their heads on the table and slumbered soundly. The Queen fell asleep over her sewing, the cook dropped off with his head in a bowl of bread dough. The cat and the dog, the page boys and the serving maids, even sparrows in the courtyard—all went sound asleep. And the minute the Princess pricked her finger, a huge wall of thorns grew up around the castle, shutting it off entirely from the rest of the world.

A new king from a far-off country came to rule the land,

and by and by nearly everyone forgot what lay behind the wall of thorns and only knew that it was a dense forest through which no one dared to make his way. However, an old woman remembered the sleeping Princess, and this woman told her daughter, who told her daughter, who told her daughter—who happened to become the nurse in the royal palace.

Exactly one hundred years to the day after the Princess had fallen into the enchanted sleep, the nurse told the Prince, who was a handsome young man by now, the story of what lay behind the wall of thorns.

"I shall waken this Princess," the Prince cried.

He went to the castle grounds. Immediately the thorny wall parted as though it had been expecting him. The Prince went on into the castle. Such a place! Dust a foot thick! And everyone asleep! The Prince went through room after room and finally came to the place where the Princess lay.

He was so entranced by her beauty that for a moment he just stood looking down upon her. Then he stooped and gently kissed her.

Immediately she opened her eyes and said, "My Prince! I have waited so long for you."

With these words the whole castle woke. The King went on with his conference, the Queen took up her sewing, the cook shaped the bread dough into loaves, the page boys and serving maids went about their business, and the birds began to sing. As for the Prince and the Princess, they were deeply in love and wanted to be married at once. And so they were; and in after years they became King and Queen and ruled the land wisely and well.

The Straw, the Coal, and the Bean

FAR AWAY and long ago there lived a poor old woman, who had gathered a big dish of beans to boil for her soup. She built a fire upon the hearth, and to make it burn quicker, threw on a handful of straw. As she put the beans in the saucepan, one fell out unnoticed and landed on the floor near a piece of straw. Soon afterward a glowing coal popped out of the fire and fell beside these two.

The Straw began to talk, saying, "My dear friends, where do you come from?"

The Coal replied, "By good luck I have sprung out of the fire, and if I had not jumped away in time, my death was certain. I would have been burned to ashes."

The Bean said, "I also have got away with a whole skin. If the old woman had put me in the pot with the others, I would be nothing but soup by now."

"I would have had no better fate," said the Straw, "for the old woman has snuffed out all my brothers. By good luck I slipped between her fingers."

"What shall we do now?" asked the Coal.

"I think," answered the Bean, "since we have so luckily escaped death, we should join in partnership and keep together like good companions. We might as well see something of the world, so let us wander forth and travel into a strange country to see the sights."

89

This suggestion pleased the others, and the three set out together on their travels. Presently they came to a little stream over which there was no bridge, and they did not know how they could cross to the other side.

The Straw said boldly, "I will stretch myself across, so that you may walk over on me. I fancy I'll make a fine bridge."

So the Straw stretched itself from one bank to the other, and the Coal, who was also of a bold nature, tripped lightly onto the makeshift bridge. But when the Coal came to the middle and heard the water rushing beneath, it was frightened and stood still, not daring to budge an inch farther. The Straw, quite overcome with so much heat all in one spot, began to burn, broke in two, and fell into the stream. As the Straw gave way, the Coal slipped after it. For a moment it hissed and spluttered and then sank beneath the waves.

The Bean, which had wisely remained upon the shore, laughed to see its bold companions in such a fix. It laughed so hard that it burst itself. And that would have been the end of the Bean if a tailor had not come along just then. Having a generous heart, he took out a needle and thread and sewed the Bean together. The Bean was grateful and thought itself as good as new.

But, as the tailor used black thread, every Bean since that time has a black seam.

King Thrush-Beard

A CERTAIN KING had a daughter who was beautiful beyond dreams, but so extremely proud and haughty that no suitor was good enough for her. She not only refused to marry every man who came to her, but she also poked fun at them.

The King was anxious to get the girl married before her bad manners became so widely known that no man would have her. So he held a feast and invited all the marriageable young men from far and near.

When they arrived they all stood in a row, according to their rank. First stood the Kings, then the Princes, the Dukes, the Earls, and last of all the Knights. Then the King's daughter was led down the rows. But she found something wrong with each man. One was too fat. "Old winetub!" said she. Another was too tall. "He'd make a better fishing pole than a husband," she giggled. A third was too short. "Half-a-man," she teased him. And so she went on, nicknaming every one of the suitors.

She made particularly merry with a young King on whose chin a mere wisp of a beard had just begun to grow.

"Ha, ha!" laughed she. "He has a beard like a thrush's beak." And after that day he went by the name of Thrush-Beard.

However, when the old King saw his daughter making fun of all the suitors, he became very angry and swore that

91

she would marry the first decent beggar who came to the gate.

A few days after this, a musician came beneath the windows to sing and so earn a few pennies. As soon as the King saw him, he ordered him to be called into the palace. The beggar came into the room in his dirty, ragged clothes and sang before the King and Princess.

When he had finished he bowed low and said, "A few pennies, your Majesty, if my song pleases."

The King said, "Your song pleases me so much that I shall give you my daughter for a wife." The Princess was terribly angry and stormed and wept, but the King said, "I have taken oath that I will give you to the first decent beggar, and I intend to keep my word."

All her tears and temper were in vain, and the Princess was married to the beggar-musician. When the ceremony was finished, the King said, "I cannot allow a beggar and his wife to remain in my palace. So be off, the both of you."

The beggar led the Princess away, and she was forced to trudge along with him on foot. As they came to a large forest she asked, "To whom does this beautiful forest belong?"

An echo replied, "To King Thrush-Beard, the True! Were you his bride, you'd rule it, too."

"Ah, how silly I was!" said she. "What a life would have been mine had I but married King Thrush-Beard!"

Next they came to a meadow, and she asked, "To whom belongs this green meadow?"

The echo answered as before, "To King Thrush-Beard, the True. Were you his bride, you'd rule it, too."

Then they came to a great city, and she asked, "To whom does this town belong?"

And the echo answered as before.

"Ah, what a simpleton I was," sighed the poor Princess.

"Why didn't I marry him when I had the chance?"

"Fie!" exclaimed the beggar. "Shame on you for always wishing for another husband. Am I not good enough for you?"

Finally they came to a very small hut, and the Princess said, "Ah, mercy, to whom can this miserable hovel belong?"

The beggar replied, "That is my house."

The hut was so small that the Princess was obliged to stoop to get inside. She asked, "Where are the servants?"

"Servants!" exclaimed her husband. "You must do all the work here."

The Princess knew nothing about making fires or cooking, and so the beggar had to set to work himself. As soon as they had finished their scanty meal, they went to bed. In the morning, the beggar awakened his wife very early, so that she might clean the house. For a few days they lived this way.

Then the husband said, "Wife, we can no longer go on without earning a penny. You must weave some baskets."

He went out and cut some willows and brought them home. But when his wife tried to make them into baskets, the twigs cut her hands and made them bleed.

"I see that won't do," said her husband. "You had better try spinning."

The Princess sat down to spin, but the harsh thread cut her tender fingers so that they bled.

"Lackaday!" said the husband. "You can't do a thing, can you? I made a bad bargain in taking you! Now we must try to make a living by selling earthen jars and dishes. You will sit in the market and sell them."

The first time she went to market, all went well, for the people bought the Princess's wares because she was so pretty. On her earnings, the beggar and she lived for some time.

When the money was gone, her husband bought a fresh

stock of dishes, and with these she again went to the market and took a stall at the corner. Suddenly a drunken soldier came plunging down the street on his horse and rode into the midst of her dishes, shattering them into a thousand pieces.

When she told her husband what had happened, he scolded her and said, "Whoever would have thought of sitting at an open corner to sell dishes? I see that you are not fit for any ordinary work. But stop crying. I have been to the King's palace, and they have agreed to take you as a kitchen maid. There you can get your own food and bring me some as well."

So the Princess became a kitchen maid. She was obliged to fetch and carry as the cook bade her and scour dirty pots and pans. She kept a jar in each of her pockets, and put into them whatever food was left from the King's table. On this she and her husband made their meals. She soon got over her pride and haughtiness and became meek and good-tempered.

About this time she heard that the King was to be married, and she begged the cook to let her watch the celebration. The cook consented and the kitchen maid placed herself near the door of the ballroom. When she saw all the guests in their fine clothes, she wept bitterly and thought how she might have been in the ballroom among them, if only she had not been so proud and haughty.

Presently the King entered, clothed in silk and velvet and wearing a golden chain round his neck. As soon as he saw the beautiful kitchen maid standing at the door, he seized her by the hand and asked her to dance with him. She was terribly frightened and tried to pull away, for she saw it was the same King Thrush-Beard who had courted her, and at whom she had laughed. Her struggles were of no avail, and as he drew her into the ballroom the jars fell out of her pockets and crashed to the floor, scattering bits of pie, cake, and meat scraps all around her.

When the guests saw this, they burst into laughter, and the poor girl was so embarrassed that she wished she had never left the kitchen. At last she managed to free herself and run off, but King Thrush-Beard soon overtook her and held her fast in his arms.

"Look at me," he said in a gentle voice. "Don't you know your own husband?" And when she stared at him wildly he added, "Yes, King Thrush-Beard and the beggar-musician are the same man. I was also the soldier who broke your dishes. I did this to help you overcome your pride and haughtiness."

At these words the Princess wept bitterly and said, "I am not worthy to be your wife, for I have been a wicked and foolish maiden."

But he replied, "Those evil days are over."

Immediately bridesmaids took the Princess away, bathed her in milk and seafoam and dressed her in beautiful clothes. Then her father and his whole court arrived and wished her happiness on her wedding day. So commenced the Princess's true joy as Queen of the handsome King Thrush-Beard.

The Brave Little Tailor

ONE SUMMER MORNING a little tailor sat upon his work-table sewing industriously. He became hungry and, going to the cupboard, got himself a piece of bread and jelly. Because he was anxious to finish the waistcoat before the end of the day, he took a bite or two of the bread and then put it down and went on with his work.

In the meantime the smell of the sweet jelly filled the air, and flies descended in swarms.

"Oh! Who invited you?" asked the little tailor, and he seized a strip of cloth and struck out fiercely. Upon counting, he found before him no less than seven dead flies. "What a brave fellow I am," he said, admiring himself. "The whole world must know this."

Quickly cutting himself a belt, he stitched upon it in large letters: *Seven at one blow!*

The tailor fastened the belt round his waist and determined to show it to the world. Before he left, however, he looked around the house for something to take with him. He found nothing except a cheese and a tame pigeon. He put these into his pocket and started out.

The road led over a mountain, and when the tailor reached the top, he saw a powerful giant. The tailor approached him and spoke to him, saying, "Good day, comrade. I am on my way to try my fortune. Would you like to go with me?"

The giant looked scornfully at the little tailor and replied, "You jack-in-the-box! You miserable do-nothing!"

"That is as it may prove," said the tailor, unbuttoning his coat and displaying the belt. "Come, read here what sort of man I am!"

The giant read, "Seven at one blow!" He thought it meant seven men whom the tailor had killed, and was greatly astonished. Wanting to test the tailor's power, the giant took a stone and squeezed it until a drop of water fell out.

"Now, do that," said the giant, "if you are so strong."

"Only that!" said the little tailor. "That is child's play!" He thrust his hand into his pocket, pulled out the cheese, and pressed it until the whey ran out.

The giant, who was quite nearsighted, thought the cheese was a stone and could hardly believe the little fellow was so powerful. The giant picked up another stone and threw it into the air. It went so high that the tailor could scarcely follow it with his eye.

"Now," said the giant, "do better!"

"That's quite a trick," said the tailor. "But your stone has returned to earth. Now, I will throw one so high that it shall never come down again." Putting his hand into his pocket, he drew forth the bird and tossed it into the air. The bird flew up, and of course did not reappear.

"What do you think of that?" asked the tailor.

"You certainly throw well!" returned the nearsighted giant. "Now we will see how you are at carrying." He then led the tailor to an enormous fallen oak.

"If you are strong enough," he said, "help me carry this tree out of the wood."

"Gladly," answered the little man. "You take the trunk on your shoulder, I will carry all the branches and twigs."

The giant took the trunk on his shoulder. But the tailor hopped up on a branch and rode along, whistling merrily.

Not being able to see around the huge trunk, the giant un-knowingly did all the work, even to carrying the little tailor. The giant, however, soon found the burden too heavy, and cried out, "Stop! I must let the tree fall!"

The tailor sprang nimbly off, seized the tree with both arms as if he had been carrying it, and said to the giant, "What, a great fellow like you not able to carry a tree?"

They left the oak where it fell and continued on their way till they saw a cherry tree growing by the wayside. The giant seized the top of the tree where the ripest fruit hung, bent it down, handed it to the tailor and bade him eat. Just as the tailor took hold, the giant let go. The bent tree sprang back into place and the little tailor was tossed up and over and landed on the other side.

"Ha!" roared the giant. "Don't you have the strength to hold down a mere bush?"

"Oh, I have strength," replied the tailor. "I jumped over the tree on purpose. Jump over it yourself, if you can."

The giant gave a leap, but one foot caught in the branches. So again the little tailor had the better of him.

Then the giant said, "As long as you are such a brave fellow, come into our cave and spend the night with me and my six brothers." The tailor was willing, and followed him to the cave. There he found six giants seated by the fire. After supper the giant pointed to a huge bed and told the tailor he might take it for the night. But it was much too big for him so he curled up on a pillow in the corner.

Just before daybreak, the giant, supposing the tailor to be asleep in bed, took an iron bar and beat the bed till the bedclothes were in ribbons. Then, sure he had killed this dangerous man, the giant and his brothers went to the wood.

Before long who should come along but the tailor, whistling merrily as if nothing had happened. Sure now that he would kill them all at one blow, the giants took to their heels, and the tailor saw them no more.

The little man went on and, after traveling a long time, came to a royal palace. Feeling extremely tired, he lay down on the grass in the courtyard and fell asleep. While he lay there, people came by and read his belt, "Seven at one blow!"

"Ah!" they said. "What a great soldier this is!" And they hurried to tell the King. The King thought such a powerful fighter would be useful in case war should break out, and he sent one of his courtiers to ask the tailor to take command of the army. The courtier stood patiently waiting till the tailor awoke, and then he delivered his message.

"That is why I am here," replied the little tailor, who by now was quite convinced of his own bravery and had completely forgotten that the seven he had killed had been only flies. "I am quite ready to take command."

Now the King's generals were jealous of the little tailor and wished him a thousand miles away.

"What can be done?" they said. "If we begin a quarrel with him, and get to fighting, he can slay all seven of us at once. We cannot risk that." So they went in a body to the King and asked to be discharged.

"We are not able," they said, "to stay in the same army with a man who kills seven at one blow."

The King was sorry that all his old and faithful officers wanted to leave him. He wished that he had never beheld the stranger, but he did not dare to discharge him, for he feared that the tailor would kill him and all his people, and then take possession of his kingdom.

At last the King thought of a plan whereby he might get rid of the fellow. So he sent for the tailor and told him that in a large wood nearby lived two giants who had committed many murders and robberies. No one dared go near them. If the tailor could conquer and kill these giants, the King would give him his only daughter in marriage and half the kingdom as a wedding present.

"Well," thought the tailor, "for such a one as I, a King's beautiful daughter and half a kingdom is not bad. I do not have such an offer every day!"

So he replied, "I will soon overcome the giants. Surely if I can settle seven at one blow, I need not fear two!"

The little tailor set out, followed by a hundred horsemen, but at the edge of the wood he said to them, "Wait here for me. I shall be better able to encounter the giants alone." Then, walking quietly, he looked about, and after a while discovered the giants. They were lying asleep under a tree.

The tailor filled both his pockets with stones and climbed the tree. He placed himself on the branch directly over the sleepers and let one stone after another fall upon the breast of one of the giants. The giant sputtered and grumbled for some time. At last he awoke, pushed his companion, and said to him, "Stop hitting me!"

"You're dreaming," said the other. "I haven't touched you."

They lay down again, and this time the tailor dropped a stone on the second giant.

"What is that?" he cried, waking with a start. "Keep your hands off me."

"I haven't laid a finger on you," said the other.

They grumbled and quarreled for some time. But they were both tired and soon went back to sleep. As soon as they began snoring again, the tailor took out a bigger stone and hit the first giant on the chest.

"Ouch!" yelled the giant. Springing up like a madman, he threw himself on his companion and tried to tear him to pieces. They rolled back and forth in their rage, uprooting trees, and fighting until they both lay dead on the ground.

The tailor now came down from his hiding place.

"What luck," he said, "that they did not tear up the tree in which I was seated." Drawing his sword, he stabbed each of the giants and then went to the horsemen, saying, "Well, that job is done. But what a time I had! The giants tore up the trees to defend themselves. But that does little good against a man like me, who kills seven at one blow."

The horsemen rode into the wood to see for themselves. There they found the giants, and all around lay the trees torn up by the roots. So they had to believe him.

The little tailor now claimed the promised reward; but the King pretended there was still more to the bargain.

"Before you marry my daughter and obtain half the kingdom," he said, "you must perform another task. You must capture a unicorn which runs wild in the wood."

"I fear the unicorn less than I did the two giants," boasted the tailor. "Seven at one blow is my motto." Taking a rope and an ax, he went in search of the unicorn.

The creature soon appeared and charged upon the tailor. The little man sprang behind an oak, and the unicorn, who was going too fast to stop, lunged against the tree and buried his horn in the trunk so deeply he could not free it.

"Ah!" said the tailor. "Now I have you." And he tied the legs of the unicorn together so it could not run away. Then he split the trunk with his ax, released the horn, and led his captive to the King.

The King, however, would not yet allow the tailor to marry the Princess, but told him he must catch a wild boar which had destroyed much property.

"Well," said the tailor, "that is child's play. Let us go at once." He would not take the hunters with him but went alone. When the wild boar saw the tailor, he rushed toward him with tusks gleaming, but the little tailor was too quick for him. He ran into a woodcutter's hut that was near and leaped through a window at the other end. The boar was on his heels, and the tailor, running round to the front door, closed it, and so the animal was caught.

The hero went at once to the King, who was now compelled to keep his promise and deliver both his daughter and half his kingdom to the tailor. The marriage was celebrated with magnificence and the tailor became a King.

One night the young Queen heard her husband talking in his sleep, and caught the words, "Sew . . . waistcoat. . . . Finish these trousers. . . . Give me the yardstick." Then she knew that her husband had worked for a living and was not suitable to be a King. She complained to her father the next day, begging his help in getting rid of this husband, who was nothing but a tailor. The King comforted her and bade her leave her door open the next night.

"My servants will wait outside," he said, "until he is asleep. Then they will tie him up in a sack and carry him off to a ship. You shall be troubled by him no more!"

The young Queen was pleased to hear this. But the tailor's page boy overheard the plot and told his master.

"Never fear," the tailor said. "I will spoil their plan." And he went to bed as usual. When the Queen thought he slept, she softly arose and opened the door. But the little tailor was only pretending sleep, and he began to call out with a loud voice, "Here, boy, sew this jacket! Mend these trousers or I will beat you with the yardstick! I have slain seven with one blow, killed two giants, captured a unicorn and a wild boar. Why should I be afraid of those who are waiting outside my door?"

When the servants heard these words, great fear seized them. They ran away as if wild beasts were after them, and no one else ever dared go against the tailor. So the tailor remained a King, and in time his wife grew fond of him, and they ruled happily for many years.

The Three Spinners

THERE WAS ONCE a lazy girl who would not spin. No matter what her mother said, she would not work. At last the mother, angry and impatient, struck the girl on the side of her head, making her cry out loudly.

Just at that moment the Queen was passing in her carriage. She heard the noise and stopped the carriage. Going up to the house, she asked the mother why she was beating her daughter. The mother was ashamed to have her daughter's laziness known, and answered, "I cannot make her stop spinning. She wants to spin all day long, and I am so poor that I cannot buy enough flax."

To this the Queen replied, "I am never more pleased than when I hear the spinning wheels whirring. Let your daughter go with me to the castle. I have flax enough, and she may spin as much as she pleases." The mother agreed, and the Queen took the girl home with her.

As soon as they reached the castle, the Queen led the girl to three rooms filled from top to bottom with the finest flax.

"Now spin this flax for me," said the Queen, "and when you have spun it all, you shall have my eldest son for a husband. Although you are poor, your eagerness to work is worth more than gold."

The girl was terrified at these words. She had not the

faintest notion how to spin flax, and could not do so if she sat there for a hundred years. But she said nothing.

When she was left alone, she began to cry, and thus she sat for three days and three nights without stirring a hand. On the fourth day the Queen came and, seeing that nothing had been done, she began to wonder about the girl. The maiden was afraid to tell the truth and excused herself by saying that she had not been able to start spinning because she was so upset about leaving home.

The Queen was sorry for her, but as she left she said, "Put your sadness behind you. You must begin your work for me tomorrow." The girl would have done so if she could, but alas, she didn't know where to start.

As she stood looking out the window, she saw three women walking past. The first had a broad flat foot, the second had such a large underlip that it nearly reached her chin, and the third had a very wide thumb. They stopped beneath the window and, looking up, asked the girl why she looked sad. She told them her trouble, and they offered her their help, saying, "Will you invite us to your wedding feast and not be ashamed of us? Will you call us your aunts and let us sit at your table? If you promise, we will spin the flax for you very quickly."

"With all my heart I will do everything you ask," replied the girl. "Come in, and begin at once."

The three women entered and, making a clear place in the first room, they sat themselves down and began spinning. One drew the thread and trod on the wheel with her broad flat foot, the second moistened the thread with her thick underlip, and the third twisted it against her wide thumb. And as they worked, pile after pile of the finest thread fell on the floor.

When the Queen came to visit, the girl hid the three spinners from her, and the Queen admired the piles of yarn and praised the girl's industry. When the first room was empty, the three women went to the second, and from there to the third room. In a very short time the flax in all three rooms was spun into the finest thread.

When their work was finished, the three spinners took their leave, saying to the girl, "Do not forget what you promised us."

When the Queen came and saw the three empty rooms and the great pile of thread, she began to plan the wedding.

"I have three aunts," said the girl, "who have been so kind to me I would not like to forget them in my good fortune. Please allow me to invite them to the wedding and to sit with me at the table." The Queen granted her wish.

The feast had just started when the three spinners entered and the bride said, "You are welcome, dear aunts."

"Oh," said the bridegroom, "where did you find such ugly relatives?" And going up to the one with the big foot, he asked, "Why have you such a broad foot?"

"From treadling, from treadling," she answered, shaking her head sadly.

Then he went to the second and asked, "Why have you such a large lip?"

"From licking, from licking."

He asked the third, "Why have you such a wide thumb?"

"From twisting thread, from twisting thread."

At this the Prince was horrified, and said, "Then my bride shall never touch another spinning wheel as long as she lives." And so she was set free for all time from the hated task of spinning flax.

The Dancing Princesses

IN A FARAWAY LAND there once lived a King who had twelve daughters, each one more beautiful than the last. They slept in twelve beds placed side by side in a long hall. Every night the King himself locked and bolted the door so they could not leave during the night, for his daughters were so beautiful that he wanted to keep them by his side forever.

But each morning when the door was unlocked, the King found that the soles of his daughters' shoes were worn as thin as paper, as if they had been dancing all night. How this could happen, neither he nor any of his wise men could imagine.

One day the King issued a proclamation that whoever could find out how the Princesses wore out their shoes should have one of the Princesses for a wife, and become King of the country. But if a person tried to find out and in three nights could not do so, then he would lose his ears.

Princes and noblemen came from far and near to try their luck, but they had no luck at all and had to go home without a wife and without ears as well. Then it happened that a wounded soldier came to town. Just outside the town gate he met an old woman chasing a pig and having a terrible time trying to catch it. In spite of his wounded leg, and although he was almost as old himself as the woman, the soldier was a nimble fellow, and he soon caught the pig.

"Thanks, many thanks," said the old woman. "Is there any help I can give you in return?"

"Well," said the soldier jokingly, "you might tell me how the twelve Princesses dance holes in their shoes every night. Then I'll become King, and won't that be a wonder!"

Much to the soldier's surprise, the woman took him seriously and said, "That task is not as difficult as you might think. Just remember not to drink the wine they give you at bedtime, and to make believe you are asleep." Then she gave him a cloak. "This cloak," she said, "will make you invisible and you can follow the maidens without being seen."

The soldier thanked the old woman and went to the palace and offered to spy on the Princesses. He was taken at once to the room adjoining their bedroom and told to keep a sharp watch if he wanted to keep his ears.

At bedtime the eldest Princess brought him a goblet of wine. He remembered the old woman's warning and, when the Princess was not looking, he threw the wine out of the window. Then he lay down and soon pretended to snore.

The twelve Princesses heard him and the eldest said, "Sound asleep and snoring. We'll fool him as we did the others."

But the soldier was not asleep. He was watching the Princesses through a crack in the wall. Just as the clock chimed twelve, the Princesses got up, dressed themselves in gowns of silver that shimmered like moonbeams, and fastened on their silver slippers. They were having a gay time—all but the youngest and most beautiful.

"Something is wrong," she said. "I feel it in my bones."

"Pooh—your bones," said the eldest. "What is there to be afraid of? I have given the soldier a drink that will keep him snoring till morning."

Then she went to the head of her bed and knocked on it three times. A door opened and the Princesses went down the stairs one after the other. The soldier put on his invisible cloak and followed them, slipping in behind the youngest Princess.

In his haste, he accidentally stepped on her dress.

"Who stepped on my dress?" she exclaimed in fright.

"Don't be silly," said the eldest. "You just caught it on a nail or something."

When they reached the bottom of the stairs, they came out on a pathway bordered with trees, the leaves of which were silver and gold that flashed and sparkled in the light.

The soldier reached up and broke off a twig to take back.

As the twig snapped, the youngest Princess called out, "Listen! Someone is following us. Did you hear that noise?"

But the eldest silenced her, saying that it was only the wind blowing through the trees.

They went on and soon came to an avenue of trees covered with leaves of diamonds. The soldier again broke off a sample, and the youngest Princess jumped in fear, but the eldest again assured her it was nothing but the wind.

At the end of the avenue they came to a lake, and on the lake were twelve boats in the shape of swans. Holding the oars of each boat was a charming Prince. As soon as they saw the Princesses, they came to shore, and each Prince took one of the Princesses in his boat with him.

The soldier stepped into the boat with the youngest Princess. As the Prince began to row, he remarked, "How heavy the boat seems tonight. I wonder why."

"The heat—perhaps," said the Princess, but she looked over her shoulder nervously.

On the other side of the lake the soldier saw a beautiful castle. From it came the most beautiful music he had ever heard. The minute the boats touched the shore the Princes and Princesses were up and away, dancing to the music.

The old soldier had never seen anything so graceful and charming. He could not help clapping his hands, and although he remembered and stopped almost at once, the youngest Princess heard him. But as usual the eldest quieted her, and they all danced on. When the first birds awoke, the Princesses stopped dancing. But by this time their shoe soles were as thin as paper.

As they reached the top of the staircase, the soldier slipped past them; and when the Princesses peeked into his room, he was snoring loudly. They took off their lovely frocks, kicked their shoes under the beds, and fell sound asleep.

The next morning the soldier said nothing of what he had seen, so that he might watch the lovely dances on the second and third nights. Everything happened just as it had the first night, except that on the third night the soldier brought back a goblet from the castle.

When the time came for him to go to the King, he hid the twigs and the goblet beneath his coat, for well he knew that he would need proof of such a tale as he must tell. It was lucky he did, for the King did not believe him. But when the soldier drew forth the twigs of gold, silver, and diamonds, the King knew he had the truth of the matter.

Then the King ordered all twelve daughters to come before him. They knew the truth was out, and they denied nothing.

"Which daughter do you wish as a wife?" the King asked. The old fellow thought a minute. "They'd make better daughters than wives to a graybeard like me," he said. "May I ask another reward instead?"

"Name it," said the King.

"Well," said the soldier, "it's this: I'd like to see your twelve daughters (and they're the loveliest in the world) marry those twelve handsome Princes they dance with so gracefully."

"Granted," said the King.

And so married they were, and the old soldier danced at the wedding.

Clever Gretel

THERE WAS ONCE a cook named Gretel, who was so fond of eating that she often ate the best things herself and served her master what was left over. But he was quite absentminded and never noticed. One day her master invited a gentleman to dinner and told Gretel to cook two fine chickens.

At the proper time, oozing gravy and done to a turn, the chickens came out of the oven. But the guest had not arrived. The master, becoming impatient, walked down the street to see if he might be able to hurry his friend's coming.

As soon as he was out of the house, Gretel put the pan with the birds to one side and said to herself, "I have been standing near the fire so long that it has made me quite thirsty. While I am waiting for the company, I may as well run to the cellar and have a little drink."

When she returned to the kitchen, she again placed the fowls on the fire and basted them with butter.

"The master would never miss a little piece," she said to herself. Then she dipped her finger in the dripping-pan to taste, and cried, "Oh, how delicious! It's a shame that there is no one here to eat them."

She ran to the window to see if her master and the guest were coming, but no one was in sight. She went and stood by the fowls and thought, "The wing of that fowl is burned a little. I had better eat it." So she cut it off and ate it. It tasted so good that she tried the second one.

After the two wings were eaten, Gretel again went to look for the master, but there was no sign of him.

"Who knows?" she said to herself. "Perhaps the visitor is not coming at all." So she went back to the kitchen and ate the remainder of the first fowl.

Now there was only one fowl left, and when her master did not return, Gretel began to look at it with longing eyes. At last she said, "Those fowls belong together; it is only fair that where one is, the other should be." She looked out the window. Seeing neither master nor guest, she ate the second fowl. Just as she was enjoying the last morsel, her master came hastening home.

"Hurry, Gretel," he called. "My guest is coming."

"Yes, master," she replied. "Dinner will soon be ready for you."

Meanwhile, the master took the carving knife and went out to sharpen it on the grindstone. While he was doing so, the guest arrived and knocked at the door. Gretel ran out to see who it was.

When she saw the visitor, she placed her finger on her lips and whispered, "Shsh! Go back as quickly as you came. If my master catches you, you'll be in a terrible fix. He invited you to dinner this evening just so he could cut off your ears. Listen, you can hear him sharpening his knife at this very moment."

The guest heard the whirring grindstone and hurried away as fast as he could. Then Gretel ran screaming to her master.

"Alack! Alas! You invited a fine guest. He came here and stole the two roast chickens. There he goes running down the street with them."

The master rushed after the "thief," knife in hand, crying,

"Stop! Stop! Let me have *one* anyway."

The guest thought he meant one *ear* and, running faster than ever, he reached home and bolted his door securely behind him.

Riquet-With-the-Tuft

ONCE UPON A TIME there lived a little Prince named Riquet, but everyone called him Riquet-with-the-Tuft, because he had been born with one little tuft of long hair on his head. He was extremely ugly, but a good fairy, feeling sorry for him, granted that he would always have good sense and be so charming that everyone would like him in spite of his looks. She also granted that when he grew up, he would have power to give equally good sense to the girl he wished to marry.

About the same time, the Queen of a neighboring kingdom had twin daughters. One girl was very beautiful but unusually stupid, while the other was very homely, but extremely clever.

The Queen sent for the same fairy who had given Riquet-with-the-Tuft his power, and asked her if she could give a few brains to the beautiful daughter. The fairy told the mother she could do nothing for the girl except to bestow on her the power to make beautiful the person whom she decided to marry.

"As for the other daughter," said the fairy, "she will be so clever and witty that no one will notice how homely she is."

As the two Princesses grew up, everyone in the kingdom talked of the beauty of the elder and the good sense of the younger. Sad to say, the beautiful one grew more stupid each day. Soon everyone deserted her for her sister, who was always witty and entertaining.

One day when the beautiful Princess was walking alone in the wood, she met an ugly little man who was richly dressed. It was Riquet-with-the-Tuft. He had seen the lovely girl's picture and had immediately fallen in love with her. Riquet recognized her at once, and asked her why she seemed so sad.

"Beauty," said Riquet, "is the greatest of all gifts. I do not see how one so beautiful can be so troubled."

"That's all very well," said the maiden, "but I would rather be as ugly as you and have some good sense."

"If that is all that is troubling you," said Riquet, "I can easily put an end to your sorrow. I have the power to give wit and good sense to the one I love. And I have loved you, dear Princess, since the first moment I saw your picture. You shall be the brightest and cleverest woman in the land, if you will only promise to marry me at the end of a year."

The Princess consented readily, for she was so stupid that a year and a lifetime seemed the same to her. Besides, she trusted that something might happen before the year was over to prevent her marriage to such an ugly person.

No sooner had she promised to marry Riquet than she felt a strange power come over her. She rushed back to the castle and gave her father such good advice that he began consulting her on affairs of state. She became so wise and said such clever things that her fame spread through the country, and all the Princes in the neighborhood wished to marry her.

Now there was one Prince who was rich, witty, and handsome, and he asked the Princess to marry him. She walked into the wood to think the matter over. She was greatly surprised to hear a babbling of voices and see dozens of little men running along with bundles under their arms.

"Where are you going, good sirs?" she asked.

"To Riquet-with-the-Tuft," they told her. "We are bearing gifts, for tomorrow is his wedding day."

All at once the Princess remembered that tomorrow was the end of the year and that she herself was to be Riquet's bride. And just then Riquet appeared.

"Ah, Princess!" he cried. "You have remembered your promise and have come to meet me."

"Oh, indeed I have not," replied the Princess. "Surely you will not hold me to a promise made when I was so stupid."

"Do not refuse me, beautiful one," said Riquet. "Do you not see that you will take away all the happiness of my life? Tell me frankly, is there anything about me that you dislike besides my ugliness?"

"No, truly," replied the Princess. "I like everything about you, except—except your looks."

"Then I need not lose my happiness, for the same fairy who gave me the gift of making you clever also gave you the gift of being able to make the man you marry handsome. Don't you think you could learn to love me enough to do that?"

He looked at her so pleadingly that the Princess was filled with pity.

"Of course I can, dear Riquet," she said, and she wished eagerly that he might become the best-looking man in the world. At once Riquet stood before her tall and straight, with dark wavy hair and flashing white teeth.

He asked the Princess to marry him and she agreed immediately. So they were married, and great was the joy of the people at having two such wise and handsome rulers.

Snow-White

ONE DAY in winter a certain Queen sat by a window sewing. As she looked out at the snow, she pricked her finger, and three drops of blood fell upon it. She gazed thoughtfully at the red drops and said, "I wish my little daughter may be as white as the snow, as red as blood, and as black as the ebony window frame."

Not long after this a baby was born to the Queen, and the child's skin was as white as snow, her lips as red as blood, and her hair as black as ebony. The Queen called her Snow-White. But sad to say, the Queen became ill and died.

The next year the King married another woman who was very beautiful, but so proud and selfish that she could not bear to think of anyone in the world being more beautiful than herself.

Her greatest treasure was a magic mirror in which she used to look and say:

> "Mirror, mirror on the wall,
> Who is the fairest one of all?"

And the mirror would answer:

> "The Magic Mirror tells you true,
> The fairest in the land is you."

As the years passed, Snow-White grew more and more

beautiful and when she was seven years old, she was fairer than the Queen herself. Then one day, when the Queen went to consult the mirror as usual, it answered:

"The Magic Mirror tells you true,
Snow-White is lovelier than you."

When the Queen heard this, she turned pale with rage and envy. Calling a huntsman to her, she said, "Take Snow-White into the forest and kill her and bring her heart back to me."

The huntsman took Snow-White into the forest, but when he lifted his sword to kill her, she begged him so sweetly to spare her life that he could not bear to touch her.

"I cannot hurt you, pretty child," he said, "but neither can I take you back, for the Queen will kill us both." So he left her in the forest, and he killed a deer and took the deer's heart to the cruel Queen.

Poor Snow-White wandered on alone, not knowing where to seek shelter. Toward evening she spied a little cottage and went in to rest herself. Everything about the cottage was small but very neat and clean. On the table was spread a white cloth and there were seven little plates, seven little forks, seven little knives, seven little spoons, and seven little mugs. Against the wall stood seven little beds.

As she was very hungry, Snow-White ate and drank, taking a little from each place, so as not to eat up all the food from any one. After that she thought she would lie down, so she tried each of the little beds. One was too long, and another too short, another too hard and another too soft, but at last the seventh suited her, and she lay down and fell fast asleep.

Presently, the masters of the cottage came home. They were seven little dwarfs who worked in the mountains digging gold. They lighted their seven lamps and saw immediately that all was not right.

The first said, "Who has been sitting on my stool?"

The second, "Who has been eating from my plate?"

The third, "Who has been nibbling my bread?"

The fourth, "Who has been cutting with my knife?"

The fifth, "Who has been using my fork?"

The sixth, "Who has been eating my porridge?"

The seventh said, "Who has been drinking my milk?"

Then the first one looked around and said, "Who has been lying on my bed?"

The rest came running to see, and each in turn cried out that somebody had been on *his* bed. Then the seventh dwarf saw Snow-White and called his brothers to come quickly. They held their lamps high so they could see better and when they saw Snow-White they cried in one voice, "What a lovely child!" They were delighted with her beauty, and took care not to waken her. The seventh dwarf slept with his brothers, an hour with each, so that Snow-White might sleep on undisturbed.

In the morning Snow-White awoke. At first she was afraid of the little men. But they were kind to her, and she soon overcame her fear and told them her story. Taking pity on her, the dwarfs said that if she would keep the house in order, cook and wash for them, she could stay in the cottage, and they would take care of her. Snow-White agreed.

Every day the dwarfs went out to their work, seeking gold and silver in the mountains. Snow-White remained at home, and every day the dwarfs warned her, "The Queen will soon find out where you are; so take care and let no one in."

The Queen, now that she thought Snow-White was dead, believed that she was certainly the loveliest lady in the land. Going to her looking glass, she said:

"Mirror, mirror on the wall,
Who is the fairest one of all?"

The glass answered:

"The Magic Mirror tells you true,
Snow-White is lovelier than you.
She's living still in forest glen,
And dwells with seven little men."

Then the Queen was mad with rage, for she knew that the mirror always spoke the truth. She knew that the huntsman had betrayed her. She could not bear to think that anyone lived who was more beautiful than she was, so she disguised herself as an old woman peddler, and went over the hills to the place where the dwarfs lived.

She knocked at the door and cried, "Fine wares to sell!"

Snow-White looked out the window and said, "Good morning, good woman. What have you to sell?"

"Good wares, fine wares," the old woman answered. "Laces and ribbons of all colors."

"I'll let the old lady in," thought Snow-White. "She seems to be an honest soul." So she unbolted the door.

"Bless me!" said the old woman. "How loosely your bodice fits! Let me lace it with one of my new laces."

Snow-White did not dream of any harm coming to her, and she let the old woman do as she wished. She pulled the lacing so tight that Snow-White lost her breath, and fell down as though she were dead.

"That will put an end to all your beauty," said the spiteful Queen, and hurried away.

When the dwarfs returned home that evening, they were grieved to see Snow-White stretched out on the floor motionless. They lifted her up, and when they found the trouble,

they cut the lacing. In a short while she began to breathe, and soon came to life again.

Then the dwarfs said, "The old woman was the Queen herself. Be more careful next time and do not let anyone in while we are away."

When the Queen got home, she went straight to her mirror and spoke to it as usual. To her great surprise it said:

> "The Magic Mirror tells you true,
> Snow-White is lovelier than you.
> She's living still in forest glen,
> And dwells with seven little men."

The Queen was furious when she heard this and, dressing herself in a different disguise, she poisoned a comb and started again for the dwarfs' cottage. When she reached there, she knocked at the door and cried, "Fine wares to sell!"

Snow-White called out, "I dare not let anyone in."

Then the Queen said, "As you like. But just look at my beautiful combs." Then she took the poisoned comb and gave it to Snow-White. It looked so pretty that she took it and put it in her hair just to try it, but the minute it touched her head she fell down senseless.

By good luck the dwarfs returned early that evening, and when they saw Snow-White lying on the floor, they could guess who had been there. They found the poisoned comb, and when they took it away, she recovered.

They warned her once more not to open the door to anyone.

Meantime, the Queen went home to her mirror and trembled with rage when it still told her that Snow-White lived. Then she said, "Snow-White will die if it costs me my life."

She secretly prepared an apple, one side of which was poisoned. Whoever tasted it was sure to die. The other side of the apple was harmless. Then the Queen dressed herself as a peasant's wife, traveled over the hills to the dwarfs' cottage, and knocked at the door.

Snow-White put her head out of the window and said, "I dare not let anyone in, for I promised the dwarfs."

"Do as you please," said the woman. "But at any rate take this pretty apple. I shall give it to you as a present."

"No," said Snow-White. "I dare not take it."

"You silly girl!" answered the woman. "What are you afraid of? Do you think it is poisoned? Come, you eat one half, and I'll eat the other."

Snow-White was tempted to taste it, for the apple looked ripe and juicy, and when she saw the woman bite into it, she, too, took a bite. She had scarcely put the piece into her mouth, when she fell down upon the floor.

"This time nothing will save you," muttered the Queen.

She went home to her mirror and asked the usual question. And the mirror answered:

> "The Magic Mirror tells you true,
> The fairest in the land is you."

Then her envious heart was glad, for she feared Snow-White no more.

When the dwarfs returned, they found Snow-White lying on the floor. No breath passed her lips, and they were afraid that she was dead. They lifted her up, combed her hair, washed her face with wine and water; but all was in vain. Snow-White did not move.

They laid her on her bed, and all seven watched over her for three days. She looked so lifelike that they put her in a glass coffin so that they might still look at her. They wrote her name on it in gold and placed it on the hill, and one of the dwarfs always sat by it and watched.

Thus Snow-White lay for a long, long time, still looking as though she were asleep. At last a Prince came through

the woods and saw Snow-White. He fell in love with her at
sight and begged the dwarfs to give her to him. Then he
offered the dwarfs money, and earnestly prayed them to let
him take her with him. But they said, "We shall not part
with her for all the gold in the world."

At last, however, they took pity on him and consented.

He called his servants to lift the coffin, and in doing so
one stumbled and fell. This jolt knocked the piece of apple
from Snow-White's mouth, and she awakened, crying out,
"Where am I?"

The Prince answered, "You are safe with me." Then telling her what had happened, he said, "I love you better than
all the world. Snow-White, please come to my father's palace
with me and be my bride."

Snow-White consented and went home with the Prince.
His parents loved her at once, and everything was prepared
for their wedding with great pomp and splendor.

Among the rest, Snow-White's old enemy, the wicked
Queen, was invited to the feast. As she was dressing herself
in fine rich clothes, she looked in her mirror and said:

>"Mirror, mirror on the wall,
>   Who is the fairest one of all?"

And the glass answered:

>"The Magic Mirror tells you true,
>   The bride is lovelier than you."

When she heard this, the Queen turned red with rage,
but her envy and curiosity were so great that she could not
resist going to see the bride. When she saw that it was no
other than Snow-White, who she thought had been dead
for a long time, she choked with passion, fell in a fit and
died.

But Snow-White and the Prince lived long and reigned
happily over their land for many, many years.

The Blue Light

THERE WAS ONCE a soldier who had served the King faithfully for many years. When peace was proclaimed, the selfish, ungrateful King said, "You can now go home. I have no more use for your services. I cannot give you any more wages, for I pay only those who are working for me."

The poor soldier did not know what to do, for he could not live without work or money, so far from home. He started out on the journey to his home village, and on the way he passed through a forest. When darkness fell and he was still in the forest, he saw a light shining through the trees. On going closer, he discovered that it came from the window of a small cottage.

He went to the door and rapped. The old witch who lived there opened the door a crack and peered out.

"Please give me a bed," he begged her, "and something to eat and drink, or I shall die of hunger."

"I will take you in if you will do whatever I wish," answered the witch.

"What is that?" the soldier asked cautiously.

"Tomorrow you must dig my garden," the witch replied.

The soldier was glad to work for his lodging and he consented. All the next day he worked hard digging the garden. He did not finish until late in the afternoon and then he was so tired he could not begin his travels again. So he begged the witch to keep him another night.

The witch consented, but she said, "If I give you lodging, you must cut this pile of wood into small pieces for my fire."

The soldier promised and he chopped wood all day. That night he was very tired and again the witch consented to give him lodging for the night.

"I have another task for you tomorrow," the witch said. "I want you to go down into the dried-up well behind the house and get my blue light for me. I dropped it into the well some time ago and have not been able to recover it."

The next day the witch led him to the well and lowered him in a basket. He soon found the blue light and gave the signal for her to draw him up. Just as he reached the edge she held out her hand to take the light. But the soldier saw that she wanted to take the light and get rid of him by letting him stay in the well.

"No," he said. "I'll not give you the light until I have my feet safe on the ground." The witch then lost her temper and let him and the light drop back into the well again.

Down, down he went and landed with a thump on the bottom. Luckily he did not hurt himself. The blue light still burned but that was of small comfort, for how could he climb up the steep sides of the well? He could see nothing ahead of him but slow death. He sat down and thought sadly of the mean trick fate had played on him.

Scarcely daring to hope, he felt in his pocket for his pipe. Ah, wonders! There it was, half filled with tobacco. "At least I shall have this last enjoyment," he said to himself. He drew out the pipe and lit it with the blue light.

As the smoke rose from the pipe, a small black man appeared and said, "Sir, what are your orders?"

The soldier was so astonished he could not utter a sound.

"It is my duty to do all you ask," the little man continued.

"Oh!" said the soldier, getting his breath at last. "Get me

out of this well at once, if you please."

The little man took him by the hand and led him through a long underground tunnel, the very place where the witch's gold was stored. The soldier carried the blue light with him, and spying the gold, gathered up as much as he could carry.

When at last the little man led the soldier up above ground, the soldier said, "Go get the old witch and bind her hand and foot and take her to the judge."

The little man vanished but soon reappeared in a puff of smoke. At the same instant a great screeching was heard. There through the air flew the witch bound hand and foot to a broomstick.

"The judge will give her what she deserves," said the little man. "Have you any further orders?"

"There is nothing more just now." The soldier thought a minute and said, "Go home, but be ready when I need you."

"You have only to light your pipe with the blue light," the little man said, "and I shall be here at once."

Instantly he vanished.

The soldier went on to the next town. He went to the finest inn and ordered the best room. Then he lit his pipe with the blue light and called the little man to him.

"I served the King faithfully," the soldier said. "But he sent me away to starve. Now I wish revenge."

"What do you want me to do?" the little man asked.

"Go to the palace during the night and bring back the King's daughter to be my maidservant," the soldier said.

"That is not hard for me to do, but it is dangerous for you, if anyone should discover you," the little man warned.

Just as the clock struck twelve, the little man brought in the King's daughter.

"Ah, there you are," said the soldier. "Fetch the broom and sweep the room."

When the Princess had finished sweeping, the soldier called her to him and ordered her to take off his boots and polish them. She did everything without a sign of resistance. Her eyes were half closed as she worked. As the cock crew, the little man appeared and took her back to the palace and to her own bed.

In the morning she told her father that she had had a very strange dream.

"I dreamed I was whisked through the streets and taken to a soldier's room," the Princess said. "There I was made to sweep the floor and polish the soldier's boots. I know it was only a dream, but I am as tired as though I had actually done the work."

The King was greatly worried. "Fill your pocket with peas tonight," he said. "Then make a tiny hole in your

pocket. If you are really taken from the palace, the peas will fall on the street and show us where you have gone."

While the King was talking, the little man stood nearby, quite unseen, and heard all that was said. That night he again whisked the Princess away from the castle and carried her to the soldier's room. The peas dropped from her pocket all along the way, but the sly little man had been there beforehand and had strewn peas over all the streets.

The Princess was made to work like a servant-maid all night and at dawn she was again returned to the castle.

In the morning the King sent out his men to follow the trail of peas, but it was a fool's errand, for all through the town the poor children were gathering peas by the handful.

"It must have rained peas last night!" they cried.

The King was more puzzled than ever and said, "We must think of another plan. When you go away tonight, hide one of your slippers in the room where you are taken. Then I will have my servants search the town for it."

The little man heard the plan, and that night when the soldier requested that he bring the Princess again, he said, "I am baffled this time. The Princess has special shoes and I can get none like them. If this shoe should be found in your room, it would go hard with you."

"Do as I tell you," the soldier answered. "I want the Princess brought here."

So for a third night the Princess was whisked away to the soldier's room and made to work. Before she left the apartment in the morning, she hid her shoe under the bed.

Immediately the King sent servants out to search the town and find the shoe. They searched and searched. They finally found the Princess's shoe under the soldier's bed. The soldier, acting on the little man's advice, had hurried out of town, but he was soon overtaken and cast into prison. And, alas, he had forgotten the blue light in his hurry! He had also forgotten to take a supply of the witch's gold, and had only a few coins.

As he looked out of his prison window he saw one of his old comrades going by. He rapped on the window and when the man came close, he said, "If you will go to my room at the inn and bring the bundle I left there, I will give you something for your trouble."

The man went quickly, and in no time at all he was back with the bundle, and the soldier paid him. As soon as the soldier was alone again, he lighted his pipe with the blue light. The little man appeared.

"Don't be afraid," the little man advised. "You will be called before the judges. Go calmly, but do not forget to carry the blue light with you."

The next day the soldier was called before the judges. But the judges would not allow him to speak in his own defense, and he was commanded to be hanged. As he walked toward the gallows he asked the King to grant him one last favor.

"What sort of favor?" asked the King.

"I wish to smoke my pipe on the way."

"You may smoke three pipes if you wish," the King said, for he could see no harm in granting the soldier's last request.

The soldier took out his pipe and lighted it with the blue light. No sooner did the smoke begin to rise than the little man appeared with a huge stick in his hands.

"What are your orders, master?" he asked.

"Strike down the false judges," the soldier commanded.

The little man swung his club with a will. Soon the judges lay on the ground. The King begged for mercy, and in order to save his life, he promised to give his daughter and his whole kingdom to the soldier.

So the brave soldier married the King's daughter and for many years they lived happily and ruled the kingdom well.

The Emperor's New Clothes

LONG, LONG AGO there lived an Emperor who loved new clothes more than anything else in the world. He cared nothing for his Army or royal balls or drives in the parks or anything else except as an excuse for showing off his fine clothes. He had a new costume for each hour of the day.

His empire was ruled by his ministers, while he spent his time before the mirror.

One day there arrived at the palace some men who claimed to be famous weavers. Now they were nothing of the kind, but only sly scalawags who made their living by cheating others. But they told of the wonderful cloth they could weave —cloth so wonderful that clothes made from it could be seen only by persons who were wise and honest. It was completely invisible to all those who were stupid or unfit for their office.

"Hm!" thought the Emperor. "Those clothes will be just the thing for me. With them I will be able to tell who is unfit for his office. No matter what the cost, I must have some clothes from that material."

Accordingly he paid the two scalawags a large sum of money, and they began their work. In a room of the palace they set up two looms. Then they ordered a great deal of the finest silk thread, and some of gold and silver. When it arrived they put it in their bags and set to work at an empty loom. They worked from morn till night, with the looms clacking away, but not a bit of cloth appeared.

The Emperor, eager for his new finery, wished to know how the work was progressing. But down in his heart he was afraid. What if the material was invisible to him? Then the people would know that he was either stupid or unworthy of being Emperor. At last he decided to send his wisest minister. Surely *he* would be able to see the cloth and report to him just what the pattern was like.

The minister hurried to the room where the weavers were working at an empty loom. Of course he could not see a thing.

"Oh, dear me!" he thought. "Am I after all such a dunce that I should not be counselor to the Emperor? I have surely tried to be a help to him. I had no idea that I was either stupid or unworthy to keep this position!"

He took off his spectacles and cleaned them. But it did no good. He didn't see a single thread. But he didn't want to lose his high position. So he made believe he could see the material very well, and he admired it, saying he liked the blending of the colors, and the delicate design.

"Do you like the unusual way in which we have combined the gold and silver in the pattern?" asked the two, and the minister assured them that he had never seen anything like it.

They told him that they could not go on without more money, as well as more of the costliest yarns. Whereupon the minister told the Emperor he should indeed grant all they asked, as the fabric was of a beauty almost unbelievable.

As before, the sly fellows put the money and the thread into their pockets, and continued to work with an empty loom.

Now the Emperor sent another wise statesman to observe the work. This man entered the room, and he almost fainted at sight of the empty loom.

"Ah!" he thought. "I cannot be stupid, surely. It must be

that there is another who could do my work better than I, and so I am unworthy of the office which I hold. Alas, that this should happen to me!"

But he never let on that he could not see any cloth. Putting on his spectacles, he moved closer to the loom, exclaiming in wonder at so fine a piece of goods. The weavers, feverishly working at their empty looms, stopped long enough to point out certain exceptional features in their masterpiece. Then they hurried on with it, saying that the Emperor wished to have it as soon as possible.

Now the news that two people had seen and admired the magical cloth began to leak out, and the whole town was filled with curiosity. And many worried for fear that at last their stupidity and unfitness for office would be found out.

One day the two weavers approached the Emperor, saying, "Sire, your fine fabric is nearly finished, but we need more money to buy some very special yarns. Would you like to come and view the unfinished cloth, so that if you are dissatisfied, you need not spend any more on it?"

The Emperor and a few of his courtiers went to the weaving room, and all stood flabbergasted when they saw only air where cloth should be. But, since none wished to let the others know, each said to his neighbor:

"Oh, see the lovely blending of colors there in the middle!"

"Surely no sunset could rival the beauty of that coloring!"

"Truly the men are artists. I wish I had some of their work."

But of course not one of them could see any colors, or any cloth, beautiful or otherwise.

The Emperor decided to wear his new clothes in a parade the next week. Thus all the townspeople could observe him in his finery, and know he was a clever and capable ruler.

The weavers cut and sewed the "material," using only

their imaginations for needle and thread, and pretended to fit the garments on the Emperor. He stood before the mirror to admire his clothes and asked, "Doesn't it fit well? Ah, yes, very nice." He went on, mumbling anything at all, so that no one would realize that he saw nothing.

"The cloth is as light as shadows, your Majesty," said one of the scalawags. "You'll think you haven't a thing on."

"Ah, yes," said the bewildered Emperor. "Very fine, very fine, indeed!"

And the scalawags laughed behind their hands.

Now the day the procession was to be held, the streets were lined with townspeople who wished to view the Emperor's new clothes. At the appointed time he appeared—walking, that the people might see him better. He was surrounded by courtiers, and two page boys held up his long train—or at least they took a firm grip on the air where they thought the train should be.

On came the Emperor, wearing not a stitch of clothing! The people gasped, but quickly made believe it was a gasp of delight at the Emperor's costume. Not for worlds would they have their friends and neighbors know their stupidity made the cloth invisible to them.

At last a little boy, too young to understand, cried out, "Why the Emperor isn't wearing any clothes!" And the people said, "You see, a little child is not wise enough to see them!" But then the people began to wonder, and all at once they all cried out, "But the Emperor is not wearing any clothes!"

And they all began to laugh!

The Emperor felt a shiver run up his backbone, for he had begun to suspect that they were right. But he could not admit it until the parade was over. So he stood all the taller and held his head high, while the page boys kept a firm hold on nothing and strutted along behind.

The White Snake

VERY LONG AGO there lived a King who was famed for his wisdom. Nothing was unknown to him, and it seemed as if he had secret knowledge of the most hidden things.

He had one curious custom. Every day after dinner, when the guests had left, a trusted young servant brought him a covered dish. Even the servant did not know what was in it. Indeed, no one knew, for the King never uncovered it until he was alone.

One day as the young servant carried away the dish, he felt a great curiosity to see its contents. Not being able to resist, he carried the dish into his own room. After carefully locking the door, he raised the cover and saw a white snake lying in the dish.

Upon looking at it, he felt such a desire to taste it that he cut a small piece and put it into his mouth. Scarcely had it touched his tongue when he heard a curious whispering of soft voices by his window. He leaned out to listen and discovered that it came from the sparrows, who were talking with each other about all they had seen in the woods and fields. Then the servant realized that tasting the snake had given him the power to understand the speech of animals.

Now it happened that, on this very day, the Queen lost her favorite ring. The King sent for this trusted servant and accused him of stealing the ring, since he was the only one to have the key to the royal jewel box. Furthermore, the King threatened that if the ring were not back the next morning, or if the servant could not prove that someone else had taken it, he would be put to death.

The servant pleaded his innocence but in vain. The enraged King all but kicked him out of the room. In his distress and embarrassment, the youth went down to the courtyard, wondering how he could escape death on the morrow. He saw some ducks swimming about in the pond, preening their feathers while they talked with each other.

The servant stopped to listen to them, and heard one tell how the sweetest water lily roots grew on the other side of the pond. Another sorrowfully remarked that he had a terrible pain in his chest, for he had swallowed a ring along with some fruit that lay under the Queen's window.

Instantly the servant seized the duck by the neck, carried it into the kitchen, and said to the cook, "Kill this duck and cook it for dinner. See how fat it is."

"Ah!" replied the cook, pinching its breastbone. "He is a plump one, all right. He'll make good eating." The duck was killed, and inside, as the servant expected, the Queen's ring was found. The servant was now able to prove his innocence to the King, and the King, wishing to make up for having so unjustly called the man a thief, allowed him to ask for any favor that he wanted.

The servant asked only for a horse and some money, for he had a desire to see the world. His request was granted and he set off down the road.

Soon he came to a pond where he saw three fish caught in a pipe and gasping for water. Having the magic power to understand all creatures, the servant knew at once what the fish wanted. Being a gentle soul, he got down from his horse and put the three captives back into the water. They splashed about joyfully and, stretching out their heads, cried, "We will remember you and repay you for saving us."

He then rode on. After a while he seemed to hear a voice among the sands at his feet. He listened and heard the King of Ants complaining.

"I wish people with their awkward animals would not step on us. That horse, with his heavy feet, treads all my people to death without any mercy." Hearing this, the servant led his horse aside and the King of Ants called to him, "We will remember you and repay you."

The road now lay through a wood. There he saw a pair of ravens standing by their nest, and throwing out their helpless young ones.

"Get out!" they exclaimed. "We cannot satisfy you, and you are big enough to feed yourselves!"

The poor creatures lay on the ground, flapped their baby wings, and cried, "See how helpless we are! We are left to feed ourselves, and we cannot fly yet. Nothing is left for us but to die of hunger." Then the good youth alighted, killed his horse with his dagger, and left it for food for the young ravens, who said, "We will think of you and repay you."

The servant was now obliged to use his own legs. After walking a considerable distance, he came to a large town. There he found great noise and excitement in the streets. A man on horseback rode about the city proclaiming:

"The King's daughter seeks a husband! But whoever desires to gain the honor of her hand must first submit to a severe trial. Should he fail, his life is forfeited."

Many men had already attempted to win the Princess, but had failed and forfeited their lives. Not daunted by this fact, the youth appeared before the King and proposed himself as a suitor for the Princess's hand. The King had no intention of letting a mere servant win his daughter and he determined to make the tests impossible.

The King and his soldiers led the servant to the seashore.

Before his eyes, they cast a ring into the waves. The King then bade him descend to the bottom of the sea and bring back the ring, saying, "If you rise to the surface without it, you must dive again, and this must be repeated until life ceases."

The townspeople pitied the handsome youth, but the King's word was law, and so they departed, leaving the young man alone on the seashore. He stood there for some time considering what he should do, when suddenly he saw three fish swimming toward him. To his astonishment, they were the same fish whose lives he had saved. The middle one held an oyster in his mouth, which he dropped at the youth's feet. When the shell was opened, the gold ring was found inside.

Full of joy, the servant returned the ring to the King, expecting that the promised reward would be given to him. But the haughty Princess, learning that he was not of equal rank with herself, did not want to marry him, and demanded that he should first submit to another trial.

She went into the garden and with her own hands strewed ten sackfuls of millet seed on the grass.

"Tomorrow, before the sun rises," she said, "all this must again be put back in the sacks. Not a grain must be missing."

The youth sat in the garden all night not knowing how he was to start the undertaking. As daylight dawned, however, he saw with amazement all ten sacks standing nearby, already filled. The Ant King had come during the night with thousands and thousands of his people, and the grateful creatures had picked up the millet seed and filled the sacks. At the appointed time the Princess entered the garden and saw the full sacks.

Still she did not want to marry the servant. So she said, "He may have accomplished two trials, but I cannot consent to have him for my husband until he brings me a golden apple from the tree of life."

The youth did not know where such a tree grew, but he resolved to search for it as long as his legs would carry him. He wandered through three kingdoms, and toward the close of a weary day's travel, he found himself in a forest. Lying down beneath a tree, he prepared to sleep. Suddenly he heard a rustling among the branches, and a golden apple fell into his hand.

At the same moment three ravens flew down and, perching themselves on his knee, said, "We are the three young ravens you saved from hunger. We heard that you were seeking the golden apple, so we flew over the sea to the end of the earth, where the tree of life is, and have brought you the apple."

Filled with joy, the young man returned to the Princess and delivered the apple. Being unable to make any further excuse, she became his bride. They shared the golden apple of life between them, and were filled with love for each other, and they lived together for many years in undisturbed happiness.

The Golden Goose

THERE WAS ONCE a man who had three sons, the youngest of whom was named Duncecap because he was so foolish. One day the eldest son wished to go into the forest to chop wood. Before he went, his mother gave him a fine large cake and a bottle of wine to take with him.

Just at the edge of the forest, the eldest son met an old man who bade him good day and said, "Give me a piece of your fine large pancake and a sip of your wine, for I am very hungry and thirsty."

But the greedy youth would not give him a bite, saying, "If I give you my cake and wine, I shall have nothing left for myself. No, indeed! Be off with you."

He left the man there and went on. He began to chop down a tree, but he had not made many strokes before he missed his aim, and the ax cut his arm so deeply he was forced to go home and have it bound up.

So then the second son went into the forest, and his mother gave him, as she had given the eldest, a fine cake and a bottle of wine. The same little old man met him and asked for a piece of his cake.

The second son likewise refused, and said, "I have scarcely enough for myself. Go, take yourself off!"

So saying, he left the old man there and went on. But he had made only two strokes at the tree when he cut his leg, and was obliged to return home.

Then Duncecap asked his father to let him go and chop wood, and his father said, "No, if your clever brothers have hurt themselves chopping wood, you would likely kill yourself." But Duncecap begged and begged and at last his father consented.

His mother gave him a crust of bread and a bottle of sour beer, thinking that the stupid boy would not know the difference. As he entered the forest, the same old man greeted him, and said, "Give me a piece of your cake and a drink from your bottle, for I am hungry and thirsty."

Duncecap answered, "I have only a hard crust and a bottle of sour beer. But if they will suit you, let us eat."

They sat down, and as soon as Duncecap touched his bread, it was changed into a fine cake, and the sour beer became wine. The two ate and drank, and when they had finished, the little old man said, "Because you have a good heart, and have willingly shared what you had, I shall make you lucky. There stands an old tree. Cut it down, and you will find something at the roots." Then the little man left.

Duncecap went directly to the tree and cut it down. When it fell, there among the roots sat a goose with feathers of pure gold. Duncecap picked it up and carried it to an inn where he intended to stay that night, for he had decided to go into the world and seek his fortune.

The landlord of this inn had three daughters, who, as soon as they saw the goose, were simply bursting with eagerness to have one of its feathers. The eldest girl watched for an opportunity to steal one. When Duncecap had gone to bed, she crept up behind the goose and caught hold of one of the wings. But the minute she touched it she stuck hard and fast and could not pull away.

Soon the second daughter came and, seeing her sister struggling to get free, she took hold of her. The second sister

had scarcely touched the first, when she was bound fast.

At last, the third daughter came. She, too, wanted to get a feather, but the others exclaimed, "Keep away, for heaven's sake! Keep away!"

The third sister did not see why she should, and thought, "The others are getting their share. Why shouldn't I?" She started to push her two sisters aside, and at once she stuck hard and fast.

So they all had to spend the night with the goose.

The next morning Duncecap set out with the goose under his arm. Since the girls were stuck to it, he took them along, too. Down the street they went wiggling and wriggling, but they could not get free. So all three of them were obliged to trot along behind him.

In the middle of a field, the Parson met them. When he saw the girls he cried out, "For shame, you good-for-nothing girls! Running after a man like that!" So saying, he took the youngest girl by the hand and tried to pull her away. But as soon as he touched her, he also stuck fast, and was forced to follow in the train.

In a few minutes they met a young father who called, "I say, Parson! Where are you going so quickly? Have you forgotten you are to christen my son today?" He grabbed

the Parson by the sleeve, and of course stuck fast.

So the five tramped on, struggling and screaming, until they met two woodsmen with hatchets in their hands. The young father called out and begged them to come and release him. No sooner had they touched him than they stuck fast to him. So now there were seven, all in a line, following behind Duncecap and the golden goose.

By and by, Duncecap came to a city where lived a King and his beautiful daughter. Now the King was disturbed because his daughter had never laughed in her whole life. He had made a law that whoever should cause her to laugh could have her for his wife.

When Duncecap heard this he went with his goose and all his train past the balcony where the Princess sat. The three girls, the Parson, the young father, and the two woodsmen were still struggling to get free, leaping about in what looked like the silliest sort of dance. As soon as the Princess saw these seven sillies, she began to laugh, and she kept on laughing as if she were never going to stop.

Promptly Duncecap let the seven sillies go and demanded his bride. But the King was not pleased with the foolish face of his future son-in-law. After a variety of excuses, the King at last said that Duncecap must bring him a man who could drink a cellarful of wine before he could marry the Princess.

Duncecap thought of the little man, who would no doubt be able to help him. Going to the forest, he saw a sad-faced fellow sitting on a stump. Duncecap asked what was bothering him, and the man answered, "I have such a great thirst and cannot quench it. Cold water I cannot bear, and a cask of wine I soon empty, for what good is a drop to a hot stone?"

"There I can help you," said Duncecap. "Come with me and you will be satisfied."

He led the man into the King's cellar. The man drank and drank, and soon he had emptied all the wine barrels.

Again Duncecap demanded his bride, but the King made a new rule that Duncecap must first find a man who could eat a whole mountain of bread.

Duncecap again set off into the forest. On the same spot as before, there sat a man who was fastening his belt tightly about him.

"I have eaten a whole ovenful of rolls," the man said, "but what use is that when one has such a hunger as I?"

Hearing these words, Duncecap was glad and said, "Get up and come with me, and you will eat enough to satisfy you."

He led the man to the royal palace where the King had ordered a huge mountain of bread to be baked. The hungry man stood before it and began to eat. He ate and ate, and in the course of the day the whole mountain vanished.

Duncecap then, for the third time, demanded his bride, but the King began again to make excuses and desired a ship which could travel both on land and water.

"As soon as you return with that," said the King, "you will have my daughter for your bride."

Duncecap went, as before, straight into the forest, and there he found the little old man with whom he had shared his bread. When Duncecap told him what he wanted, the old man gave him a ship which could travel both on land and water. "Since I have eaten and drunk with you," the little man said, "I give you the ship. All this I do because you were generous."

As soon as the King saw the ship, he could no longer keep his daughter, and the wedding was celebrated. After the King's death, Duncecap inherited the kingdom, and lived a long, contented life with his bride.

Master of All Masters

THERE WAS ONCE a young girl who went to the fair looking for someone who would hire her as a servant. And just about that time there was an old man who went to the fair looking for someone to come and do his housework. So they met and struck up a bargain as to wages, and the girl went home with him that very day.

Now the minute they got inside the house the old man said, "Sit down, lass, and open both your ears. For in this house I have my own names for things, and you must learn to call my things by these names or else never speak. So, then, what will you call me?"

"Master—or mister—or whatever you like, sir," said the girl, feeling much bewildered.

"Nay, no," said he. "You must call me Master of all Masters. And what will you call this?" He pointed his long bony finger at the bed.

"Bed or bunk or whatever you like, sir," said she.

"Nay, no, that's my Barnacle. And what do you call these?" he replied, holding out his baggy trousers.

"Pants or pantaloons or whatever you like, sir."

"Nay, no, those are my Squibs and Crackers."

Just then the cat came into the room. "What will you call her?" asked the old man.

"Cat or kitty or whatever you like, sir."

"Nay, no. You must call her Whitefaced Siminy," said
he, and then he pointed to the fire. "That, now. What
would you be calling that?"

"Fire or flame or whatever you like, sir."

"Nay, no. You must call it Hot Cockalorum. And what is
this now?" he went on, pointing out the bucket of water
that stood in the kitchen.

"Water or drink or whatever you like, sir."

"Nay, no. That is Pondalorum. And what do you call all
this?" he asked, waving his hand to include the whole
house.

"House or home or whatever you like, sir."

"Nay, no. You must call it High Topper Mountain. And
see that you do, or else hold your tongue."

The poor girl went off to her work and served the supper
without uttering a word for fear of saying the wrong thing.
The old man ate up every bite and then went to bed and
fell sound asleep.

Suddenly the girl shook him wide awake, crying, "Master
of all Masters, get out of your Barnacle and put on your
Squibs and Crackers! For Whitefaced Siminy has got a
spark of Hot Cockalorum on her tail, and unless you get
some more Pondalorum, High Topper Mountain will be all
Hot Cockalorum!"

The Golden Bird

A LONG, LONG TIME AGO there was a King who had a fine garden adjoining his palace. In this garden stood a tree which bore golden apples. Every day the apples were counted, and one day an apple was missing.

This vexed the King greatly, and he ordered that the tree should be watched every night. He trusted no one but his own sons to do this, and on the first evening he sent the eldest to keep watch. About midnight the youth fell asleep, and in the morning another apple was missing.

The next night the second son watched, but he fared no better. A third apple was missing the next morning.

It was now the third son's turn. He was eager to go, but the King hesitated a long time, thinking the lad would be even less wakeful than his brothers. But there was no one else to send; so the youngest son went.

He lay down under the tree and watched steadily. Just as the clock struck twelve, something rustled in the air. Looking up, the boy saw a bird with feathers of shining gold. The golden bird lighted upon the tree and was just about to pick an apple when the youth shot an arrow at it.

The bird was not harmed, but one of its golden feathers dropped off as it flew away. In the morning the third son showed the feather to the King and told him what he had seen during the night. The King immediately called his council, and every member declared that the single golden feather was worth a kingdom.

"Well, then!" said the King. "If this feather is so valuable, I must, and I will, have the whole bird!"

So the eldest son was sent out in search of the golden bird. When he had walked about a mile, he saw a fox. He drew his bow to shoot, but the fox cried out, "Do not shoot me, and I will give you a piece of good advice! You are now on the road to the Golden Bird. This evening you will come into a village where two inns stand opposite each other. One will be brightly lighted and much merriment will be going on inside. Do not turn in there; enter the other one, though it may seem a poor place to you."

The young man thought to himself, "How can a dumb beast give me good advice?" Going nearer, he shot at the fox. He missed, and the fox ran away with its tail in the air.

The young man walked on and toward evening came to the village where the two inns stood. One inn was brightly lighted and sounds of dance music could be heard through the open doors. The other looked dark and dreary.

"I would be a simpleton," the young man said to himself, "if I were to go into that dirty inn." So he entered the merry inn, and there, in feasting and dancing, he forgot the Golden Bird and his father's errand.

As time passed by and the eldest son did not return home, the second son set out to seek the Golden Bird. The fox met him, too, and gave him the same advice that the eldest brother had received. When the second son reached the two inns, there was his brother leaning out of the window of the merry inn and beckoning to him. The second son went in and forgot all else in feasting and dancing.

Again a long time passed with no news of either brother. The youngest boy wished to go and try his luck, but his father would not consent.

"It is useless," said he. "You are less likely than your brothers to find the Golden Bird. Surely some misfortune would befall you." The lad continued to beg, and at last the King was forced to consent.

As the youngest son came to the edge of the forest, the fox was again sitting there. Again he offered, in return for his life, the same piece of advice.

The youth, being good-hearted, said, "Be not afraid, little fox, I will do you no harm."

"You will not be sorry for your goodness," replied the fox. "Get on my tail that you may travel quicker."

Scarcely had the lad seated himself, when away they went, over sticks and stones, traveling so fast that his hair whistled in the wind. When they arrived at the village the youth dismounted and, following the advice of the fox, he turned into the mean-looking inn, where he spent the night undisturbed.

The next morning, when he was once more on the road, he found the fox awaiting him.

"I will tell you what you must do now," said the fox. "Go straight forward, and you will come to a castle before which a whole troop of soldiers will be sleeping and snoring. Do not be frightened, but go right past them and search the castle till you come to a room where a Golden Bird hangs in a wooden cage. Nearby stands an empty golden cage, but be careful you do not take the bird out of its ugly cage and place it in the golden one, or you will fare badly."

With these words, the fox again stretched out its tail, and the King's son climbed onto it. Away they went. When they arrived at the castle, the youth found everything as the fox had said. He soon discovered the room where the Golden Bird sat in its wooden cage.

The youth thought it would be a pity to take the bird in

such an ugly, dirty thing, so he put it into the golden cage.
At the moment he did this, the bird set up a piercing shriek.
This woke the sleeping soldiers, who jumped up hurriedly
and made the youngest son a prisoner.

The next morning he was brought before the King, who
owned the bird. When the lad confessed to having taken
the bird, he was condemned to death. However, the King
said he would spare his life under one condition, namely,
if the lad brought to him the Golden Horse which traveled
faster than the wind. Then as a reward, he would receive the
Golden Bird.

The young Prince left the castle sighing sorrowfully, for
where was he to find the Golden Horse? All at once, he
saw his old friend the fox, who said, "There, see what happened because you did not obey me? But do not be discouraged; I will tell you where you may find the horse.

"Follow this road till you come to a castle; in the stable
stands the Golden Horse. Before the door, three boys lie
fast asleep; so you must lead the horse away quietly. But remember one thing: put the old saddle of wood and leather
on his back, and not the golden one which hangs close by,
or you will be unlucky."

So saying, the fox stretched out his tail, and away the
two went as fast as the wind. Everything was as the fox had
said, and the youth went into the stall of the Golden Horse.

As he was about to put on the wooden saddle, he thought,
"What a shame to put this thing on such a fine animal!" So
he took up the golden saddle instead. Scarcely had it touched
the horse's back when the animal gave a loud neigh which
awoke the stableboys. They took the young Prince and shut
him up.

The next morning he was taken before the King and condemned to death. But the King promised to give him his
life and the horse, if he would bring him the beautiful

daughter of the King of the Golden Castle.

With a heavy heart the youth set out, and in a little while he met the fox.

"I should have left you in your misfortune," said the fox. "But you were kind to me, and I am willing to help you out of your trouble once more. Your road to the Golden Castle lies straight before you. You will arrive there about evening, but wait till the Princess goes to take a bath. As soon as she enters the bathhouse, you spring up, give her a kiss, and she will follow you anywhere. Take care, however, that she does not say good-bye to her parents first, or all will be lost."

With these words the fox again stretched out his tail, and when the King's son had seated himself, away they went over sticks and stones like the wind. When they arrived at the Golden Castle, the youth found everything as the fox had foretold, and he kept out of sight until the Princess came to the bathhouse. He sprang up instantly and kissed her. The Princess said she was willing to go with him, but begged him, with tears in her eyes, to be allowed to tell her parents good-bye. At first the boy withstood her entreaties, but as she continued to weep, he consented.

But the King fell in a rage at the very thought of losing his daughter. He promptly aroused the soldiers, who captured the youth and put him in prison.

The following morning, the King said to him, "You deserve death. But since my daughter begs me to be merciful I shall give you one chance. If in eight days you can remove the mountain which lies before my window, you shall have my daughter as a reward."

Immediately the youth began digging and shoveling away, but when, after seven days, he saw how little he had accomplished, he gave up all hope.

On the evening of the seventh day the fox appeared and

said, "You do not deserve that I should notice you again, but go away and sleep while I work for you."

The lad lay down and was soon fast asleep. When he awoke the next morning the mountain had disappeared. Full of joy, he hastened to the King and told him the conditions of the pardon had been fulfilled. Now the King was obliged to keep his word and give up his daughter.

The two started off on their journey, but they had not gone far when they met the faithful fox.

"You have the Golden Maid," he said. "You must have the Golden Horse as well."

"How shall I obtain it?" inquired the youth.

"That I shall tell you," answered the fox. "First, take the beautiful Princess to the King who sent you to the Golden Castle. He will readily give you the Golden Horse in exchange for the Princess. Mount the horse and shake hands with everyone. Last of all, take the Princess's hand and swing her up behind you. Then ride off at full speed and no one can catch you, for the Golden Horse goes as fast as the wind."

These directions were followed, and the youth got the horse and kept the beautiful Princess as well. The fox, who traveled by their side, said to the Prince, "Now I will help you to get the Golden Bird. When we come near the castle, I will take the Princess into my cave. Then you ride into the courtyard, and at the sight of the horse there will be such joy that they will readily give you the bird. As soon as you hold the cage in your hand, ride off like the wind."

As soon as this deed was done, and the Prince had ridden back with his treasure, the fox said, "Now you must reward me for my services."

"What do you desire?" asked the youth.

"When we come to the forest, kill me and cut off my head and feet."

"Ah, no," said the Prince. "You have been my friend. I cannot slay you."

"If you will not do it, I must leave you," replied the fox. "But before I depart I shall give you one more piece of advice. Remember two things: buy no gallows-flesh, and do not sit on the edge of a spring!" With these words the fox ran quickly off into the forest.

The young Prince thought, "Ah, that fox has curious fancies! Who would buy gallows-flesh? And I don't see the pleasure of sitting on the edge of a spring!"

He rode on with his beautiful companion, and soon came to the inn where his two brothers had stopped. There he heard a great uproar, and he was told that two thieves were about to be hanged on the gallows. As he drew nearer, he saw that the thieves were his two brothers. He promptly paid back the money they had taken and his two brothers were released.

After this, the four set out and soon came to the forest where they had first met the fox. As it was cool and pleasant beneath the trees, the two brothers said, "Come, let us rest here by this spring, and eat and drink."

The youngest consented, forgetting the warning the fox had given him. All at once the brothers threw him backward into the spring and, taking the maiden, the horse, and the bird, went home to their father.

The brothers boasted loudly of their great skill in capturing the Golden Bird, and also the Golden Horse and the Princess.

The whole court praised them, but the horse would not eat, the bird would not sing, and the maiden did nothing but weep bitterly over the loss of her drowned sweetheart.

The youngest brother, however, was not drowned. The spring, by great good luck, was dry. He fell upon soft mud without any injury; but he could not get out again. Even now the faithful fox did not leave him, but soon came up and scolded him for not following his advice.

"Still I cannot forsake you," said he. "You were kind to me and I will again help you. Hold tight to my tail, and I will pull you up to the top." When this was done the fox said, "You are not yet out of danger, for your brothers are not sure of your death and have set guards all around the forest to kill you if they should see you."

Thereupon, the youth traded clothes with an old beggar who happened by, and in that disguise went to his father's palace. No one recognized him; but instantly the bird began to sing, the horse began to eat, and the beautiful maiden ceased weeping. Bewildered at this change, the King asked her what it meant.

"I do not know," replied the maiden, "but I was sad and am now gay, for I feel as if my true love had returned."

Then she told him all that had happened, although the other brothers had threatened her with death if she disclosed it. The King ordered everyone in the castle to pass before him and among them came the youngest son dressed as a beggar. The maiden knew him instantly. The wicked brothers were thrown into a dungeon, but the youngest son married the Princess.

One day the Prince went again into the wood. The fox met him and said, "You now have everything that you desire, but there is no end to my misfortune, although it lies in your power to release me." And with tears he begged the youth to cut off his head and feet.

At last the Prince did so, and scarcely was it done when the fox became a man. He was none other than the brother of the Golden Princess, who had long been under an evil spell. The Prince took him home to the palace, and from that time on they all lived happily.

The Frog Prince

ONE FINE EVENING a young Princess went into a wood and sat down beside a cool spring. She had her favorite plaything, a golden ball, in her hand, and she amused herself by tossing it against a tree and catching it again as it bounced back.

After a time she threw the ball so hard that, though she stretched out her hand to catch it, the ball bounced away and rolled into the spring. Then the Princess began to weep as if her heart were broken.

While she was weeping, a frog popped up out of the water and said, "Princess, why do you weep so bitterly?"

"Alas!" she said. "My golden ball has fallen into the spring. I would give all my jewels if I could have it back."

The frog said, "I do not want your jewels, but if you will love me and let me live with you, let me eat from your golden plate and sleep upon your bed, I will bring you your ball."

"Ugh!" thought the Princess. "I couldn't stand the slimy old thing." But she wanted her ball very much. So, not meaning a word of it, she cried out, "Yes, yes, I promise. Only bring me my ball!"

The frog dived deep under the water. Soon he came up with the ball and threw it on the ground. The Princess scooped it up quickly and ran home as fast as she could.

The frog called after her, "Wait, Princess! Take me with you as you promised." But she did not even turn around.

That night as the Princess sat down to dinner, she heard a strange noise, thump-thump, as if somebody were hopping up the marble staircase on one foot. Soon there was a gentle knock at the door and a voice:

"Open the door, my Princess dear,
  Open it for your lover, here.
  Remember the promise you gave to me,
  As you played with your ball 'neath the old oak tree."

The Princess ran to the door and opened it, and there she saw the frog, whom she had quite forgotten. She was terribly frightened. She slammed the door as fast as she could and came back to her place at the table. The King, her father, asked her what had frightened her.

"There is a nasty frog at the door," she said. "He brought my ball out of the spring this morning. I promised him that he should live with me, thinking that he could never get out of the spring, but here he is at the door and he wants to come in!"

While she was speaking the frog knocked at the door again.

"Open the door, my Princess dear,
  Open it for your lover, here.
  Remember the promise you gave to me,
  As you played with your ball 'neath the old oak tree."

The King said to the young Princess, "If you have made a promise, you must keep it. Go and let him in."

The Princess pouted and sulked, but she had to obey. The frog hopped into the room and came to the table.

"Pray lift me up beside you," he said to the Princess. And she had to pick up the cold, slimy creature. Then the frog said, "Put your plate closer to me so that I may eat out of it." The Princess did so unwillingly, and when he had eaten his fill, the frog said, "Now I am tired; carry me upstairs and put me into your little bed."

The Princess took him upstairs and threw him into a closet. But he cried so loudly that she had to let him out for fear her father would hear him and punish her. The frog hopped up on the pillow, where he slept all night. As soon as it was light he jumped up, hopped downstairs and out of the house.

"Now," thought the Princess, "he is gone, and I shall be troubled with him no more."

But she was mistaken, for when night came, she heard the same thump-thumping on the staircase, followed by a

tapping at the door. When she opened it, the frog came in and slept upon her pillow until morning. The third night he did the same. But when the Princess awoke, she blinked her eyes in amazement. Instead of the frog, there stood beside her a handsome Prince with the most beautiful eyes she had ever seen.

"You," she faltered, "you are the frog?"

"Yes," he said. "Your frog is a Prince." Then he told her that he had been enchanted by a witch and forced to remain a frog until some Princess should let him eat from her plate and sleep upon her bed for three nights.

"You," said the Prince, "have broken this cruel charm, and now I have nothing to wish for but that you will be my bride and go to my father's kingdom with me, for I love you dearly."

The Princess was not long in giving her consent, for a handsome husband is not to be found on one's pillow every day. Just then a splendid carriage drawn by eight beautiful horses decked with golden plumes drove up. The Prince and Princess joyfully set out for the Prince's kingdom, where they lived happily a great many years.

The Pink

THERE WAS ONCE a Queen who had never had a child. Every morning she went into the garden to pray that a son or daughter might be granted her.

One morning an angel came to her and said, "Be content, a son will be given to you, and he will be able to obtain anything he wishes for." The Queen hastened to the King with the joyful news, and before long she had a son.

Every morning the Queen went to bathe the child in a clear spring that flowed in the meadow. Now it happened that one time as the child lay upon her lap after his bath, the Queen fell asleep. An old cook, who knew that the child could have whatever he wished, came and stole him away. Then, taking a hen, he killed it, and sprinkled the Queen's clothes with the blood.

The child was carried to a secret place where the cook had provided a nurse for it. He then proceeded with the rest of his wicked scheme.

Hastening to the King, the old cook told him that the Queen had allowed the child to be carried away by wild beasts. When the King saw the bloody clothes, he believed the cook and flew into a rage.

To punish the Queen he threw her into a high tower. He ordered the entrance to be walled up and said that the Queen must stay there for seven years, without meat or drink. The King, of course, thought she would die. But two angels, in the form of white doves, came to the Queen every day, bringing everything that she needed.

In the meantime, the cook thought to himself, "The child can obtain all he wishes. I had better stay right with him." So he left the palace and, going to the boy, who was now old enough to speak, he said to him, "Wish for a beautiful palace, and everything that should belong to it." Scarcely had the boy uttered the words than everything he had named stood there.

After a while, the cook said to him, "It is not good for you to be alone so much. Wish for a beautiful maiden for a companion." The King's son did as directed, and a beautiful maiden immediately stood before him. The boy played with her in the palace gardens and learned to love her deeply.

The old cook now went out hunting like any nobleman, but he was not altogether easy in his mind, for he feared the little Prince might someday remember his father and wish to be with him. Then it would be death for the cook.

Therefore, the wicked man went out, took the maiden aside, and said to her, "This very night, when the boy sleeps, plunge this knife in his breast, and bring me his heart as a proof I am obeyed." Seeing that she hesitated, he added, "I shall kill you instantly if you refuse," and she was obliged to consent.

But the maiden could not kill her dear playmate. When the old cook had departed, she ordered a deer to be slain. Taking the deer's heart, she placed it on a plate. When she saw the cook returning, she bade the boy get into bed and cover himself with the bedclothes. When the cook asked if she had carried out his orders, the maiden presented him with the plate containing the deer's heart.

Before the cook could speak, the boy threw back the bed-clothes, and to the cook's astonishment, said, "Wicked one!

Your wickedness shall be punished! You shall become a black spaniel with a golden chain round your neck, and you shall feed upon glowing coals, so that flames pour from your throat." As soon as the words were spoken, the old cook changed into a black spaniel. Some glowing coals were brought. He devoured them, and the flames rushed forth from his throat.

Soon after this the youth remembered his mother, and he longed to know if she were still living. Therefore, he said to the maiden, "I must seek my own country, and if you will go with me, I will protect you."

"Ah," she replied, "how can I travel so far, and what would I do in a foreign land where I am unknown?" But still they did not wish to be separated from each other, so the King's son wished that she become a beautiful pink flower.

He started out for his homeland, carrying the pink with him. The spaniel followed them. Before many days' journey the youth arrived in his native land. He wished to be set down outside his mother's house. Instantly he was beside the tower where his mother was imprisoned. Then he wished for a ladder to reach the top. He mounted and, looking in, exclaimed, "Dearest mother, lady Queen, are you living or dead?"

She immediately answered, "I have just eaten and have had sufficient," for she thought the doves had spoken.

"I am your own son," answered the youth, "who was supposed to have been carried off by wild beasts. But I am living and well, and hope shortly to release you."

Then he descended the ladder and, going to the gates of his father's palace, had himself announced as a foreign huntsman, and requested to be taken into service.

The King replied, "I will hire him if the man is well skilled and can shoot a good supply of venison."

The huntsman promised to procure as much venison as would be required for the King's table. He commanded all the other huntsmen to form a circle in the forest. Then he wished that the deer should collect within the circle. More than two hundred deer appeared. They were shot down by the huntsmen.

The King was pleased and ordered a great banquet. When all the court was assembled, the King said to the huntsman, "You are so famous a hunter that you deserve to sit next to me in the seat of honor."

The youth replied, "May it please Your Majesty, I am unworthy of so great an honor, for I am only a poor huntsman."

But the King persisted, and the youth sat beside him. The boy thought of his poor mother and wished that one of the King's attendants would speak of her. Scarcely had he wished, when the King's grand marshal said, "Your Gracious Majesty, we are living here in pleasure and abundance, but how is your wife in the tower? Is she living or has she perished miserably?"

"Silence!" thundered the King. "She let my son be devoured by wild beasts. My heart is steeled to her sufferings."

Hearing this, the huntsman arose and said, "Gracious King and Father, she is still living, and I am her son. The wild beasts did not carry me away; it was that wicked wretch, your old cook. While my mother slept, he took me from her lap and sprinkled her dress with blood in order to mislead you." Then, calling the spaniel with the gold chain round his neck, the youth showed him to the King, saying, "This is the wicked brute." Sending for hot coals, he made the creature eat them.

"Now," said the youth, "behold him in his true form and believe me." The spaniel was instantly changed into the cook. The fellow's guilty look was enough to condemn him.

The King could scarcely control his rage and ordered the cook to be imprisoned in the deepest dungeon.

"Ah, my son," said the King. "What a cruel life you have led." But the youth said he had been quite happy and asked if the King would like to see the maiden who had not only brought him up tenderly, but when ordered to kill him had refused to do so.

"Yes," said the King, "I would gladly see her."

Putting his hand in his pocket, the youth brought out the pink. Everyone stared in amazement.

"Now," said the son, "I will show her to you in her true form." He wished her to be a maiden again, and she stood before them in all her beauty.

"And the Queen, my mother," said the youth. "Would you see her also?"

"Yes, yes," cried the King, and he wept bitter tears to think that he had treated her so unjustly. The Queen appeared at once and the King begged her forgiveness and heaped honors and rich gifts upon her. The young Prince married the beautiful flower-maiden and they lived happily ever after.

Beauty and the Beast

THERE ONCE LIVED a rich merchant who had three sons and three daughters. They lived happily together until one day the father received word that all his ships had been lost at sea. Every penny he owned had gone to pay for the ships' cargoes, and now there was nothing left of his fortune but an old house in the country.

The merchant was glad to have a roof over his head, but the children complained from morning till night. The boys sulked because they had to work the fields. The girls pouted because they had to work about the house. All complained but the youngest girl, Beauty. She worked with a will and was always happy and smiling.

One day the merchant received word that one of his ships had been washed ashore, and so some of his fortune had been saved. Full of high hope, he prepared at once to go to the city and sell his cargo. As he left, he asked each of his daughters what they wished him to bring them. The eldest wanted some diamonds and pearls, while the second asked for a handsome silk dress. But Beauty, thinking how much they all needed, asked only for a red rose.

The father bade his children good-bye and set out. When he reached the city, he found that some wicked men had claimed his ship and that he was as poor as ever. With a heavy heart he started home again, traveling day and night.

In the darkness he lost his way. After going miles along a deserted road, he saw at the far end of a tree-bordered lane a palace lighted from top to bottom.

"Perhaps I can find shelter here for the night," he said to himself and hurried forward.

He knocked loudly at the front door, but no one answered. Then he went around to the back door. No one opened it, either. He wandered to the stables but saw not a living soul. He went again to the front door and, finding it unlocked, he went inside.

There was no one in sight, but on the table was laid a delicious supper. The merchant was very hungry and sat down to eat. Still no one appeared, but in the next room he spied a bed and slept there for the rest of the night. In the morning he got up and started home. But just as he passed a bush of beautiful red roses, he remembered his promise to bring a flower to Beauty, and he plucked one of the roses.

The minute he touched the rose, a harsh voice called out, "Stop, thief!"

The frightened merchant turned to see an ugly beast coming toward him.

"How dare you pluck my roses?" roared the Beast. "I give you food and lodging and this is how I am repaid! You shall die for this!"

"I-I-I—" stammered the merchant, his wits leaving him. Then somehow he managed to find his tongue again. He told the Beast all about sweet, unselfish little Beauty and how she had asked for only a rose while her sisters demanded dresses and jewels.

The Beast seemed to think deeply. At last he grunted, "Go then. I shall spare your life. Take the rose, but in a month you must send Beauty to live with me."

The merchant took the rose and went sadly home.

When he had told his children that they were still poor, he gave Beauty the rose and said, "Little can you guess how much this cost me." Then he told the story of the Beast and his castle.

"Do not grieve, dear Father," Beauty said. "I will go to the castle of the Beast."

Her father and brothers would not hear of such a thing, but Beauty said, "You made a promise and I will keep it."

So when the month was over, Beauty and her father started out for the Beast's palace.

When they reached the palace, no one was in sight. They entered and found the table set for two. When they had finished eating, the Beast appeared. He greeted Beauty and her father and told the merchant that he must return home and leave his daughter in the palace.

"Have no fear," he said. "I will not harm her."

So the merchant was forced to bid his daughter good-bye and go home without her.

Beauty wandered about the palace and at length came to a door bearing a sign that read, BEAUTY'S ROOM. She entered and found the room furnished with everything a girl's heart could desire. She picked up a book, opened it, and read, "All your commands will be obeyed. You are Queen of everything in this palace."

"I wish for nothing but to see my father," the girl said to herself in a sad tone.

Lifting her eyes to the large mirror, she saw as if in a dream her father returning to his home. The vision remained in the mirror only a moment, but she was thankful to the Beast for fulfilling her wish.

That evening when she went to supper, the Beast appeared and asked if he might share the meal with her. She could not refuse, although she trembled from head to foot at his ugliness.

"Do you think I am terribly ugly?" he asked her.

"Yes, I do," Beauty answered in all honesty. "But," she added quickly, "I'm sure you have a very kind heart."

After they had finished eating supper the Beast said, "Will you marry me, Beauty?"

The girl started up in alarm, but managed to falter, "No, Beast. I cannot marry you."

The Beast sighed heavily, said good night, and left the room. Beauty said nothing, but she pitied him from the bottom of her kind heart.

For some time, Beauty lived on in the palace. All day long she saw no one, but always at suppertime, the Beast appeared. Each night he asked her to marry him, and each night her answer was no. Yet she grew to like him, for he was always kind and gentle to her.

One day when Beauty looked into her magic mirror, she found her father ill. She begged the Beast to be allowed to go to him. The Beast agreed but said that she must return within a month. If she did not return within that time, he would die. He told her that all she had to do when she wished to come back was to turn her ring on her finger three times before she went to sleep. In the morning, when she woke up, she would find herself in the palace.

The next morning Beauty found herself in her father's home. He was so happy to see her that he soon became well again. The days passed so swiftly that the month was over before Beauty realized it. Still she lingered on, saying each night, "One more day. Just one more day won't matter to the Beast."

One night she dreamed that she saw the Beast lying half dead in the garden. She woke in tears and quickly turned her ring three times on her finger. The next morning she found herself back in the palace.

The Beast was not there, but she did not expect him till

suppertime, and so she did not worry. But suppertime came and still the Beast did not appear. Beauty was overcome with grief.

"Ah, me," she cried, "I have killed him with my unkindness."

She ran into the garden in search of him and there she found him lying senseless on the ground. Quickly she brought water from the fountain and bathed his face. At last he opened his eyes and said, "You forgot your promise and I could not live without you. But I can at least die happy now, for I have seen you once more."

"No! No!" Beauty sobbed. "You shall not die, Beast. You shall live and be my husband, for now I know I love you."

As Beauty said these words, the palace sparkled with light, and sweet music filled the air. The ugly Beast vanished, and in his place knelt a beautiful Prince.

"But where is my poor Beast?" Beauty asked.

"I was the Beast," the Prince answered. "A wicked fairy bewitched me and condemned me to live in the form of a hideous beast until some good and beautiful maiden should promise to marry me in spite of my ugliness."

Then Beauty wept for joy and the Prince gathered her in his arms and carried her into the palace. There stood Beauty's father, and he gave them his blessing. The young people were married at once, and they lived to reign happily over the kingdom for many, many years.

Ali Baba and the Forty Thieves

IN PERSIA there once lived two brothers. Cassim, the elder brother, had married a rich woman and so lived in fine state. But Ali Baba, the younger brother, had married a woman as poor as himself, and he had to work hard for a living.

He had managed to scrape together enough money to buy three donkeys. Every day he drove the donkeys into a nearby forest and loaded them with firewood, which he then sold in the public market.

One hot afternoon Ali Baba had just finished loading his three beasts with their daily burden of wood, when he saw many horsemen galloping toward him.

"Ah!" thought Ali Baba. "Only thieves could be in such a hurry on a hot day. I had best make myself scarce." And so he prudently tethered the donkeys in a thicket where they could not be seen from the road and climbed a tree.

The band of horsemen came to a stop directly under the tree in which Ali Baba was hiding. As they dismounted he counted them and discovered that there were exactly forty. One of them, probably the captain, stepped up to a flat boulder on the rocky hillside and said in a deep, clear voice, "Open, Sesame!"

At once the boulder swung open like the door of a castle, and the forty thieves stepped inside. As soon as the last one had crossed the threshold, the door swung shut and not even the sharpest eyes could have told where the opening had been.

Ali Baba was trembling so that he nearly fell out of the tree, but he managed to hold on until the forty robbers reappeared. The leader said, "Shut, Sesame!" And once more the boulder swung back into place. Then the forty thieves galloped off.

Ali Baba stayed in the tree as long as he could see the least speck of dust from the galloping hoofs. When he was certain that the robbers were out of sight, he climbed down. All the while he had been saying, "Sesame, sesame," over and over to himself so that he would not forget the name of the grain that the robber chief had used as the magic password.

He stepped up to the boulder and said, "Open, Sesame!" Immediately the door flew open. Ali Baba entered and found a spacious cavern, dimly lighted from cracks in the roof, and piled high with treasure chests, sacks of gold coins, jewels, bales of rich silks, and all manner of loot that the thieves had stolen and hidden there.

Leaving the silks and jewels for a later trip, Ali Baba took only as much gold as he thought his three donkeys could carry. Once again he said the magic word and the door flew open. Quickly Ali Baba took out the firewood from the saddle baskets and put in the gold, covering it well with a few sticks of wood. Then he said, "Shut, Sesame!" as the thief had done and hurried back to town as fast as the donkeys would go.

He put the donkeys in the stable, tossed them a handful of hay, and carried the baskets into the house.

"Have you gone crazy?" demanded his wife when she saw him. "Bringing wood inside instead of selling it?"

"Hold your tongue," Ali Baba ordered. "And draw the curtains. Lock the doors."

His wife did as she was told, but when Ali Baba opened
the bags and poured out the gold in a glittering heap she
shrieked in amazement.

"Hush!" Ali Baba begged her. "Do you want the neighbors to hear?" And he warned her that they must spend
their new wealth only a little at a time so that no one
would suspect that they had found a treasure. His wife
promised, but she would not rest content until she had
found out how much gold her husband had brought.

At first she tried to count it, but the sum soon became
larger than she was able to reckon and she didn't know what
number came next. Then she thought of weighing it, but
she had no scales. So she went to the house of Cassim, her
brother-in-law, and asked his wife to lend her the scales.

Now Cassim's wife was curious as to what poor Ali Baba
could have that needed weighing. So she rubbed the bottom

of the scales with mutton fat, hoping that whatever they touched would stick. Sure enough, when the scales were returned, a gold coin was sticking to the bottom.

Cassim's wife immediately told her husband, and the two wondered about their brother's sudden wealth until they were sick with jealousy. At last Cassim could stand it no longer and went to Ali Baba and demanded to know how he had gotten so much gold that he had to weigh it.

Ali Baba saw that he would have to tell his brother his secret, and as there was easily enough treasure in the cave to make them both rich, he told him the magic word.

The next morning Cassim was up before daybreak, determined to go to the cave and get all he could before Ali Baba would have a chance. With him he took ten donkeys loaded with the biggest baskets he could find. He found the rock and, having said, "Open, Sesame!" went inside and began filling his saddle-baskets. At last they were full, but there was so much treasure left in the cave that the greedy brother wished he had brought twenty donkeys.

He was so upset about the treasure he was leaving behind that he completely forgot the magic word. All he could remember was that it was some kind of grain. So he said, "Open, Barley." But the door remained solid rock. Then he tried, "Open, Wheat." Still it stood steadfast. He tore his hair with rage, but the door would not budge.

Just then the thieves came back to the cave with more loot they had taken from some unfortunate travelers. The minute the door swung open, Cassim darted out, hoping to escape, but the robbers caught him and quickly put him to death. They hung his body inside the cave as a warning for anyone else who might know their secret, and then went on their way.

Meanwhile Cassim's wife grew worried at her husband's failure to return. At length she went to Ali Baba and told him what Cassim had done. Ali Baba warned her to tell no one, and then he set out for the cave. He found Cassim quickly enough and brought the body back with him hidden in the donkey's saddle-basket under a pile of wood.

He comforted the poor wife as best he could and told her that he and his family would come to live with her so that he could look after his brother's son and manage his affairs. The wife agreed readily, and the two households became one that very day.

In the meantime Ali Baba spoke to one of Cassim's serving-maids, Morgiana by name, who was devoted to the family and had long served them faithfully and well. Morgiana promised to devise a scheme so that no one should know that Cassim had been murdered.

Forthwith she went to a seller of herbs and powders and requested a medicine of great strength. When asked to whom this medicine was to be given, Morgiana pretended to weep bitterly and said that it was for her master, who suffered great pain and could not be expected to live until morning. In this way news of Cassim's illness was spread about, and no one was surprised to hear of his death the next day.

While all this was taking place, the thieves returned to the cave and found that both Cassim's body and more of their treasure were missing. They decided to send one of their number to the town disguised as a traveler to try to find out who had discovered their secret. This spy was to look for two things: a man who had been murdered and a man who had suddenly become wealthy. The spy soon discovered that Ali Baba was the answer to both questions, since he was newly rich and had a brother who had died after a short illness.

The leader of the band then thought of a clever scheme to get inside Ali Baba's house without arousing suspicion. He pretended to be an oil merchant and managed to reach Ali Baba's house just at sunset. Since there was no inn nearby, he asked Ali Baba to shelter him and his donkeys for the night. Ali Baba agreed, and the donkeys—each laden with huge oil jars—passed inside Ali Baba's gate. The first few jars did indeed contain oil, but inside each of the others crouched a thief.

Now it happened that Morgiana, needing some oil for a lamp, went to one of the jars and discovered the trick. She summoned another servant to help her. Working quietly, they poured boiling oil into each of the jars, thus killing the whole band of robbers except the leader, who was pretending to be asleep inside the house.

When the leader came to rouse his men for the attack on Ali Baba, he found them all boiled alive. He quickly made his escape, but he swore to have revenge on Ali Baba.

A few days later he returned to the town in a different disguise and made friends with Cassim's son, who soon invited the stranger to his house for dinner. Ali Baba did not recognize the man, but Morgiana did. And she saw that the thief had a dagger hidden inside his shirt.

As soon as dinner was over she dressed herself as a dancer and came to entertain the guest. Little did he guess what sort of entertainment she planned, for he did not see the dagger hidden beneath her sash. She flung herself at his feet as if asking for reward, and as he reached for a few coins she whirled out the dagger and stabbed him.

Ali Baba and young Cassim cried out in horror, but their horror was soon changed to joy when Morgiana showed them who their guest really was. Young Cassim was so overcome with her cleverness that he asked Morgiana to marry him at once. She consented, and the wedding was held soon.

Now that all the thieves were dead, the whole treasure in the cave belonged to Ali Baba, who, of course, shared it with young Cassim and Morgiana. They used it wisely and lived in great honor, as did their children after them.

The Lad Who Visited the North Wind

A BOY ONCE LIVED ALONE with his poor widowed mother. One day his mother sent him to the storeroom to get some flour. The boy got the flour, but as he was returning across the yard, the North Wind came blustering along and blew the flour from the dish.

The boy went to get some more flour. He was crossing the yard the second time when the North Wind whirled around the corner of the house and with one puff blew all the flour away.

The boy returned to the storeroom once more. He filled his dish with the last bit of flour and went out into the yard. Along came the North Wind, and away went the flour.

By this time the lad was angry. It did not seem right that the North Wind should have all the flour and he and his mother have none at all.

"There is nothing for me to do but to visit the North Wind and demand my flour," the boy told his mother.

So he set out. He walked and walked and walked, for the road to the North Wind was long. At length he came to the place where the North Wind lived.

"Good day," said the youth.

"Good day," roared the North Wind, who couldn't speak softly if he tried. "What do you want?"

"Please give me back my flour," said the boy. "We have

none at all, and if you do not give it back, we shall starve."

"I have no flour," the North Wind answered. "But you may have the cloth that lies in the corner. If you say, 'Cloth, spread yourself,' it will be covered with all sorts of good things to eat."

The lad was well pleased with the cloth. He thanked the North Wind and set out for home. But he had gone so far that he could not reach home in one night. So he decided to stop at an inn.

While the other guests were eating, the lad sat down at a table in the corner of the dining room.

"Cloth, spread yourself," he said, putting the cloth on the table. Immediately the table was covered by many good dishes.

The innkeeper's wife saw the magic cloth and was determined to get it, for it would be a good thing to have in her business. That night when the boy was sound asleep, she quietly took away the magic cloth and put in its place an ordinary one that looked just like it.

When the lad woke the next morning, he took his cloth and started home. He walked and walked and reached there just at dinnertime.

"Well, I have been to the North Wind," the lad told his mother. "He is a very fine person and he gave me a cloth that will furnish us with all sorts of good food. We shall never be hungry again."

"I will believe it when I see it," the mother answered.

The boy put the cloth on the table.

"Cloth, spread yourself," he said. But the cloth brought forth not even one dry crumb.

"I see I shall have to visit the North Wind again," the boy said. So he started out once more on his journey.

He walked and walked and finally came to the place where the North Wind sat.

"Good day," the boy said.

"What do you want this time?" the North Wind roared.

"I want the flour you took from me, for that cloth you gave me is worth nothing."

"I have no flour to give you," the North Wind said. "But if you wish, you may have this goat. You have but to say, 'Goat, make money,' and gold coins will fall from its mouth."

The boy thanked the North Wind and started home with the magic goat.

As the way was long, the boy could not reach home that night. So he stopped at the inn as he had done on his first trip. Before he went to bed that night, he thought he would try out the power of the goat.

"Goat, make money," he ordered.

Immediately gold coins spattered from the goat's mouth. The innkeeper thought that it would be a fine thing to have such an animal, and that night when the lad was sound asleep, he quietly exchanged the magic goat for a goat that looked exactly like him.

The next morning the boy awoke and, taking his goat with him, started for home. When he reached there, he told his mother of the fine bargain he had made with the North Wind.

"I will believe it when I see it," his mother said.

Then the boy said to the goat, "Goat, make money." But nothing at all happened.

"The North Wind has certainly cheated me again," the boy complained. "There is nothing I can do but go to see him once more."

Away the boy went again. He walked and walked and finally came to the place where the North Wind sat.

"Good day," he said.

"Good day to you," roared the North Wind. "What is

it that you want from me now?"

"I have come to get my flour back," the boy said. "The goat you gave me is no good."

"I have no flour to give you and nothing else but the stick that stands in the corner. However, it is of some worth. If you say, 'Stick, lay on,' it will beat that person until you say, 'Stick, lay off.' "

The boy picked up the stick, thanked the North Wind and started home. Again he stopped at the same inn where he had stayed before. This time he kept his stick with him, for he had begun to suspect what had happened to his cloth and his goat.

When the lad was asleep, the innkeeper came to steal the stick. He did not know what it would do, but he was sure it must be as wonderful as the goat and the cloth. Just as he was about to pick it up, the lad called, "Stick, lay on!"

The stick began to beat the man. Around the room he ran, jumping over chairs and dodging around the table, and the stick after him, whack, thwack, whack!

"Ouch," he yelled. "Oh! Oh! Make it stop, and I'll give you your cloth and your goat."

"Stick, lay off!" the lad said, and immediately the stick stopped beating the man.

The innkeeper gave the lad his cloth and his goat. Taking all three magic gifts from the North Wind, the lad started for home. Now he and his mother would never want for anything the rest of their lives.

Jorinda and Jorindel

THERE WAS ONCE an old castle that stood in the middle of a dense wood. In the castle lived a very old witch. All day long she flew about in the form of an owl, but at night she became an old woman again.

When any young man came within a hundred steps of her castle, she turned him into a statue, and he could not move a step until she set him free. But when a pretty maiden came within that distance, she was changed into a bird, and the witch put her into a cage and hung her up in a large chamber in the castle.

Now there lived at this time a beautiful maiden whose name was Jorinda. A shepherd, whose name was Jorindel, loved her dearly, and soon they were to be married. One day, the two went for a walk in the wood, and Jorindel said, "We must take great care that we do not go too near the witch's castle."

It was a beautiful day; the last rays of the setting sun shone bright on the white bark of the birches, and the turtledoves sang from the pine trees. Suddenly they looked around and discovered that they had, without knowing it, walked right under the walls of the enchanted castle.

Jorindel shrank back in fear, turned pale, and trembled like a leaf. Jorinda, all unknowing of their plight, continued the song she was singing:

> "The gray dove sings in the pine,
>   Sweetheart mine,
> He sings to his mate of their love,
>   Of their love,
>   Of their lo—"

Suddenly the song ceased. Jorindel turned and saw that his Jorinda had changed into a nightingale. With mournful tone she kept repeating her last note, "Lo-lo-lo."

An owl with fiery eyes flew round about them three times, and three times screamed, "Tu whu! Tu whu! Tu whu!" Jorindel could not move; he stood fixed as a stone, and could neither weep, nor speak, nor stir hand or foot. Now the sun had gone down, and the owl flew into a bush. A moment later the old witch came from the bush. She was pale and thin, with staring eyes and a great beak of a nose that almost met her sharp, pointed chin.

She mumbled something to herself, seized the nightingale, and went away with it in her hand. Poor Jorindel saw her take the nightingale but could do nothing about it. At last the witch came back and sang with a hoarse voice:

> "In a prison cage I've bound her,
> With my magic I'll surround her,
> Never more shall she be free,
> Hence, young lad, away with thee."

Suddenly Jorindel found himself free. He fell on his knees and begged the witch to give him back his dear Jorinda, but she said he would never see her again, and went away.

He prayed, he wept, he sorrowed, but all in vain. At last he rose and went to a nearby village, where he found work tending sheep. Every day he came as near to the hated castle as he dared and thought longingly of his lost love.

One night he dreamed that he found a beautiful purple

flower, and in the middle of it lay a costly pearl. He dreamed that he plucked the flower, and went, with it in his hand, into the castle. Everything he touched with it was disenchanted, and so he found his dear Jorinda again.

When he awoke he immediately hurried forth and searched over hill and dale for the purple flower. Eight long days he looked for it in vain. On the ninth day, just before the sun went down, he found the beautiful purple flower, and in the center of it was a large dewdrop as big as a pearl.

He plucked the flower and hastened to the castle. The magic flower protected him from the witch's power.

Jorindel touched the gate with the flower, and it sprang open. He went in through the courtyard and heard a beautiful flood of music as if hundreds of birds were singing in chorus. He followed the sweet sound and at last he came to the chamber where the witch sat. Around her were seven hundred birds in seven hundred cages, and all the birds were singing to the ugly old witch.

When she saw Jorindel, she screamed with rage and stamped her foot, but she could not come close to him because of the flower. Quickly Jorindel went from cage to cage looking for his love. But alas! There were many, many nightingales. How then, could he tell which one was his Jorinda?

While he was wondering what to do, he noticed that the witch had taken down one of the cages, and was trying to tiptoe out with it. He leaped after her, touched the cage with the flower, and lo! his Jorinda stood before him. She looked as beautiful as ever and he clasped her tenderly in his arms. At this sight the witch flew into a fit and vanished in a puff of yellow smoke.

Then Jorindel touched all the other birds with the purple flower, and each one became a beautiful maiden. He led them all to their homes. Then Jorinda and Jorindel were married and lived happily together for many years.

The Flying Trunk

THERE ONCE LIVED in a town far over the sea a merchant who was very wealthy. He was so wealthy that he could have paved the street on which he lived with golden coins and perhaps have some left over. But he made better use of his money. He would not part with a penny unless he was sure it would come back with nine others earned. So his wealth grew and grew, but finally he died and left all his money to his son.

Now when the son inherited all this money, he led a merry life. He went to parties every night and used paper money for kite tails and threw pieces of gold from his window just to see them splash in the river below. In this way his money soon disappeared and he had nothing left but four pennies and an old dressing gown. His friends turned their backs on him, for he looked very silly walking on the street in a dressing gown.

One of his friends, however, sent him an old trunk with the advice that he should pack as soon as possible. But as the merchant's son had nothing to pack, he jokingly climbed in the trunk himself.

Now this trunk was a curious one. When the lock was fastened, the trunk could fly through the air. So when the young man got into the trunk and unknowingly pressed the lock, he found himself flying up the chimney!

186

Up and up he went, higher and higher. Once in a while the trunk would creak as though it was about to break into pieces, but nothing happened. Before long the trunk came down to earth in the land where the Turks live.

The young man hid the trunk in a cave and went on into the town. He did not feel a bit out of style here, for everyone seemed to wear garments much like his dressing gown.

In the distance he saw turrets of a castle. He stopped a nurse with a little child and asked her who lived there.

"The King's daughter lives there," the woman said. "The wise men have foretold that a lover will cause her much heartache. So she lives there alone and sees no one but those persons brought by her father and mother."

The young man thanked the woman and went back to the cave. He climbed back into his trunk and flew to the castle. He landed on the roof and climbed through the window of the Princess's chamber.

The Princess was lying on her couch, and she looked so beautiful that the young man could not resist kissing her. She awoke startled, but the young man told her he was an angel and had flown down from the sky to see her. When she heard this, she felt quite honored by his company.

For a long time they sat talking. He made extravagant speeches about her eyes and her snowy forehead and her dimpled chin. Then he asked her to marry him and she immediately answered yes.

"But you must come for tea at six o'clock Saturday," the Princess said. "My mother and father will be here then. They will be flattered to have an angel for a son-in-law. But be prepared to tell us a story, for my parents love to hear stories."

"Well, I will bring a story," the young man said. "But that will be my only wedding gift." Then the Princess buckled about his waist a beautiful saber enclosed in a sheath of gold coins—and gold coins were something he could make good use of—and he climbed into his flying trunk and went away.

The young man bought himself some new clothes and spent all the week in the cave writing a story. Shortly before six o'clock on Saturday the story was finished, and he flew to the royal palace.

The King and Queen and all the court were waiting for him. He was greeted warmly and was served tea at once.

When tea was finished, the Queen said, "Now tell us your story. It must be both wise and useful."

"But let it have a bit of a laugh, too," put in the King.

So the young man told this story:

"There was once a bundle of Matches who considered themselves of very high descent. They thought themselves much better than the other kitchen folk, for they were the splinters of a monarch of the forest, a lofty pine. They still boasted of their royal descent although they had now come down in the world and were lying on a bare hearth in a kitchen between the Iron Pot and a Tinder Box.

"The Matches told how they had used to drink diamond-like dew in the morning, how the sun shone on them all day and the birds told them stories while they were green and in the forest. They were very proud because they were green all year round, while the other trees about them were quite bare in winter.

"But one day the woodcutters came and broke up the family. The head of the family, the trunk of the tree, was made into a ship's mast. The large branches were used in various ways, and the small bits became match sticks and so were banished to the kitchen.

"The Iron Pot told his story. He told how since the very beginning of his life he was continually being put in the

fire and then scoured and scrubbed.

"The Tinder Box interrupted and complained that the talk was too serious. He requested that they have a merry evening.

"So they talked of one thing and another. The Plates and Broom joined in, and the Market Basket gave the latest news of the town, for he got around more than the others.

"Then the Tongs danced, and they asked the Teapot to sing. But she refused because she could sing only when she was hot. Someone suggested that since the Teapot would not sing, they should ask the nightingale who lived in a cage outside the door to sing. But others disagreed, saying the nightingale was not one of them and should not be given such an honor.

"The disagreement grew into a quarrel and before they could settle it, the servant opened the door and everyone was as quiet as a mouse.

"The servant lighted the Matches. 'Now,' they thought, 'everyone can see how bright we are.' But in only a moment they were burned out and all was ended—and so is my tale."

"That was a splendid story," the Queen said. "There's nothing like having a good story teller right in the family. You may certainly have my daughter."

"Of course," nodded the King. "On Monday we shall have the wedding."

That night there was great rejoicing in the town. Gingerbread and all sorts of goodies were given away by the boxful, and the boys whistled and shouted for joy at the treat.

"Now, I must do my share of treating," the young man thought. He went into the town and bought all the fireworks and firecrackers he could find. He put them all in the trunk and flew up into the air.

Around and around he flew in dizzy circles, shooting off

one burst of fireworks after the other. The people down below jumped so high with joy that their slippers flew about their ears. They had never witnessed such a sight before. There was no doubt but that the young man was indeed an angel.

As soon as the merchant's son got back into the cave, he hid his trunk carefully and went into the town to see what the people were saying about his display of fireworks. Everyone whom he saw gave a different description of the show, but all agreed that they had never seen anything like it.

"I saw the angel myself," one of the men said. "He had eyes like the sparkling stars."

"He floated on a fiery cloak, and I saw the heads of cherubs peeping out," said another.

The merchant's son hurried back to the cave, happy that his spectacle had been such a success. When he reached the place where he had left the trunk, he found it gone. Nothing was left but a pile of smoldering ashes.

In his hurry to find out what people were saying about him, he had carelessly left a half-burned firecracker in the trunk and the dry wood had taken fire. Now that he could no longer fly, he could not return to his promised bride, for he dared not confess that he was only an ordinary man and not an angel after all.

The Princess stood waiting for him the whole day. She may be waiting still, while he wanders about the world telling stories, none of them as good as the one he told the King and Queen and their court.

The Goose Girl

THERE WAS ONCE a Queen whose husband had not long been dead. She had promised her daughter in marriage to a Prince in a faraway land. When it came time for the wedding, the Queen gathered together many beautiful things and gave her daughter a serving-maid and two horses to carry them on their way.

Just before it was time for the Princess to leave, her mother called her daughter to her and gave her a golden charm to wear. This charm, she said, would protect her as long as she wore it. The horse she rode, the Queen told her daughter, was a magic horse and could speak the language of human beings. The Queen tucked the charm inside the girl's dress and the Princess and her maid rode away.

As they rode along, the sun rose higher in the sky and the Princess became very thirsty. When they came to a brook, the Princess said to her maid, "Get down, I pray you, and get me a drink of water."

The maid, who was impudent and lazy, answered, "If you want a drink you will have to get it yourself! I will not wait on you."

So the Princess got down from her horse and, going to the brook, knelt down to drink.

"Alas, alas," she sighed, "what will become of me?"

The charm in her bosom answered:

> "Alas, alas, if your mother knew,
> Her loving heart would break in two."

The Princess mounted her horse and rode on. Soon she again became thirsty. As she was a kind-hearted girl, and believed no harm of anyone, she again asked the maid to get her a drink of water. Again the maid refused, and the Princess dismounted and knelt beside the brook to drink. As she did so, the golden charm slipped from her dress and floated down the stream. The Princess did not notice it, but the maid saw it and knew that she now had the Princess in her power.

When the Princess was about to mount her horse again, the maid pushed her aside.

"I will ride Falada, the magic horse," she said. "You can ride my old nag."

As the maid had already mounted Falada, there was nothing for the Princess to do but to mount the old nag. This she did, and they rode on toward the Prince's kingdom.

They had not gone far when the servant girl stopped and forced the Princess to change clothes with her. The servant girl now was dressed in the Princess's clothes and rode the Princess's horse. So it was not surprising that when they reached the palace, the servant girl was taken for the Princess, and the Princess was made to go to the servants' quarters. As the false Princess sent her away, she said, "If you speak a word of what happened on the way, I shall surely see that you will die."

The false Princess was given a royal welcome and went to dine with the Prince and his father. As the Prince looked out the window, he saw a strange servant girl wandering aimlessly about the courtyard.

"Ah, who can that be?" he said. "She is very beautiful."

"That is but a serving-maid I brought with me," the false Princess answered. "She is very lazy." Then turning to the

King she added, "I wish that you would give her some really hard work to do."

"Well, now," said the King, "she might help the gooseherd."

So it came about that on the next morning the real Princess was sent with Conrad, the gooseherd, to look after the geese.

Everything was going just as the false Princess wished. But she still feared that Falada, the talking horse, might give away her secret. So she thought of a scheme to do away with the magic horse.

"Will you do me a favor?" she asked the Prince, and smiled at him prettily.

The Prince, anxious to do anything to please his future wife, gave his promise at once.

"Kill the horse on which I rode here," she said. "He is an ill-tempered beast and will surely cause trouble if left alive."

The Prince did not like to have so handsome a creature killed, but as he had given his promise, he ordered a groom to kill Falada that very night. When the real Princess heard of this she wept bitterly and went to the groom. She offered him her only gold piece if he would fasten Falada's head to the gate through which she must pass on her way to the hills with the geese. She begged so hard that he did as she asked.

The next morning as the real Princess and the gooseherd passed through the gate, she looked up at Falada's head and said sorrowfully:

> "Falada, Falada, thou art dead,
>   And all the joy from my life is fled."

At this the head answered:

> "Alas, alas, if your mother knew,
>   Her loving heart would break in two."

Conrad and the real Princess went on into the meadow with the geese and sat down to watch them. The Princess let down her hair and the gooseherd, seeing the beautiful locks like strands of spun gold shining in the sun, tried to steal a curl. But just as his hand came near her head, the Princess said:

"Blow, wind, blow, I say,
Snatch the gooseherd's hat away.

After it let Conrad run,
While I sit here in the sun.

Let him not come back, I pray,
Till my hair is combed today."

At once the wind blew Conrad's hat away and he ran after it. He ran and ran, but he did not catch it and return until the girl's hair was neatly braided and tucked under her cap. Conrad was sulky and would not speak to her the rest of the day.

The next morning Conrad and the Princess started out as before. The Princess again spoke to Falada's head, and the head answered with the same words. When they reached the meadow, the Princess let down her hair and again Conrad tried to steal a lock. But the Princess bade the wind blow, and whisk! Away went Conrad's hat and Conrad after it.

Conrad was sulkier than before and muttered and grumbled all the day. That night when they returned to the palace, he complained to the King.

"I will not go to the meadow again with that girl," he said.

"Why not?" the King asked.

"Because all day she teases me," Conrad said. Then he told how the strange girl spoke to the horse's head each morning and how it answered her. He told, too, how she loosened her hair and then told the wind to blow his hat away.

The King was puzzled at this story, and the next morning he went to the meadows himself and hid behind some bushes. He saw the Princess loosen her hair and heard her tell the wind to blow Conrad's cap away. Then he watched her while she arranged her hair and he marveled to see how it rivaled the sun in brightness and beauty. After a time he crept away without letting anyone know he had been there.

That night he called the girl to him and asked who she was and what her strange actions meant.

"I dare not tell you," the girl answered sadly. "If I do I shall lose my life."

The King promised her that he would see no harm came to her and he looked so kind and fatherly that the girl told him her story. When she had finished, the King told her to dry her eyes and weep no more, for he would help her regain her rightful place. Then he sent for the serving-maids to dress her in beautiful clothes.

When she appeared in her royal robes it was clear that her story was true, for no one but a Princess could be so beautiful and walk with such stately grace.

That evening at dinner the King told everyone that he had to pass sentence on a wicked servant who had been false to his master and betrayed his trust.

"What do you think should be done to punish such a person?" the King asked the false Princess.

"He should be put in a dark dungeon and never allowed to see the light of day again," she answered, never dreaming that the King was speaking of her own wicked deed.

"That is the way it shall be," the King said. "You have chosen your own punishment."

So the wicked servant girl was thrown into a dungeon. As for the real Princess and the Prince, they were married at once and lived happily for many, many years.

The Coat of Many Skins

A KING once had a wife who was so beautiful that her equal could not be found in the whole world. She fell ill, and when she was about to die, she called the King and said, "You must have no Queen after my death who is not as beautiful as I or who has not golden hair like mine. This you must promise me." The King gave his promise, and she closed her eyes and died.

For a long time the King could not be comforted. Finally, his councilors said that he must marry again for the country must have a Queen. Then messengers were sent far and wide to seek a bride who was as beautiful as the late Queen. But although they searched diligently the whole world over, no one was found.

Now the King had a daughter who was as beautiful as her dead mother. She had the same golden hair, and as she grew up, the King saw how like his lost wife she was. He told his councilors that he wished his daughter to marry his oldest councilor, and that the pair should rule in his stead. When the oldest councilor heard this, he was delighted.

The daughter did not like the King's plan and hoped to turn him from it. Finally, she said to him, "Before I fulfill your wish, I must have three dresses: one as golden as the sun, another as silver as the moon, and the third as shining as the stars. Further, I desire a coat made of thousands of skins. Every beast in your kingdom must contribute a portion of his skin to make it."

The Princess thought this would be impossible to do, and so she would put a stop to her father's plan. But the King would not give up, and the cleverest maidens in his kingdom set to work to weave the cloth for the three dresses. His huntsmen were sent out to catch all the beasts in the kingdom. From each animal they were to take a piece of skin to make the coat of a thousand pieces.

At length, when all was ready, the King had the coat and the dresses brought before him and, spreading them out before his daughter, he said, "Tomorrow the wedding will take place."

When the King's daughter saw that there was no hope of turning her father from his plan, she decided to flee. That night while all slept, she took her three treasures: a golden ring, a tiny gold spinning wheel, and a gold reel. She put the three new dresses in a nutshell and put on the cloak of many skins. Then she covered her hands and face with soot and left the castle. She traveled all night, till she came to a forest, where she took refuge in a hollow tree and went to sleep.

It happened that the King who owned this forest came to hunt in it. When his dogs came to the tree in which the Princess slept, they barked and growled so that the King said to his huntsmen, "See what wild animal is concealed there."

The hunters examined the hollow and said, "In that hollow lies a wonderful creature whose like we have never seen before. Its skin is composed of a thousand different colors, but it lies quite still and asleep."

"Try to catch it alive," commanded the King. "Bind it to the carriage and take it back with us."

As soon as the hunters took hold of the maiden, she awakened. She was terrified and called out, "I am a poor child

forsaken by both father and mother! Pray pity me and take
me with you!"

Because of her mantle, they named her "Allerleirauh,"
which means "many colors," and took her home with them
to serve in the kitchen. They showed her a small room under
the stairs where no daylight could enter and told her she
could sleep there. All day she worked in the kitchen carrying water and wood, tending the fire, plucking fowls, raking
out the ashes, and doing all manner of dirty work.

One time a feast was held in the palace, and she said to
the cook, "May I look on at the feast for a little while? I
shall stand just outside the door."

"Yes," the cook replied, "but in a half-hour you must
return and rake out the ashes."

Allerleirauh went to her dark room, took off the coat of
skins and washed the soot from her face and hands so that
her real beauty could be seen. Then she opened her nutshell
and took out the dress which shone like the sun. As soon as
she was ready, she went up to the ballroom.

Everyone bowed to her, for they supposed that she was
some Princess. The King himself soon came to her and,
taking her hand, danced with her. As soon as the dance
was finished, she curtsied, and before the King could look
around, she had disappeared from sight.

The watchmen at the gates were called and questioned,
but they had not seen the maiden. She had run back to her
room, taken off her dress, blackened her face and hands,
put on the cloak of all skins, and become Allerleirauh once
more.

As soon as she returned to the kitchen, the cook said,
"Cook the King's supper for me tonight. I want to go upstairs to have a peep at the ball. But mind you, do not let
one of your hairs fall in, or you will get nothing to eat."

So saying, she went away, and Allerleirauh made some

soup for the King's supper. When it was ready she went to her room, fetched her gold ring, and dropped it into the dish. When the King tasted the soup he declared he had never before eaten anything so good. Just as he had nearly finished it, he was surprised to see a gold ring at the bottom of the dish. He commanded the cook to be brought to him.

The cook was terrified when she heard this order, for she thought something was wrong with the food.

"Are you certain you did not let a hair fall into the soup?" she asked the girl.

Then she went trembling before the King.

"Who cooked my supper?" he asked.

"I did," she answered.

"That is not true, for it is much better than usual."

Then the cook said, "I must confess Allerleirauh cooked it."

So the King commanded that the kitchen maid be brought

to him. When Allerleirauh appeared, he asked, "Who are you?"

"I am a poor child without father or mother," she replied.

The King then asked, "Where did you get this ring, then?"

Allerleirauh answered, "I know nothing of it." As she would say no more, at last she was sent away.

After a time there was another ball, and Allerleirauh asked the cook's permission to look on.

"Return here in a half-hour," the cook said, "to cook the soup for the King."

Allerleirauh ran into her dark room, washed herself quickly, took out the dress which was as silver as the moon, and put it on. Then she went up to the ballroom. The King was very glad to see her again, and since the dancing had just begun, he chose her for his partner.

As soon as the dance was over, the girl disappeared so quickly that the King did not notice where she went. She ran to her room, changed her garments again, and went into the kitchen to make the King's soup. While the cook was upstairs, the maiden dropped the golden spinning wheel into the soup and served it to the King.

The King found the soup tasted as good as that he had had before. The cook was called, and again was obliged to confess that Allerleirauh had made it. Allerleirauh was taken before the King, but she declared she knew nothing of the golden spinning wheel.

Not long afterward a third ball was given by the King. Allerleirauh asked permission to go and the cook said, "You are certainly a witch. You always put something in the soup which makes it taste better than mine. Still, you beg so hard, you may go at the usual time."

This time Allerleirauh put on the dress as shining as the stars and stepped into the ballroom. The King danced with her again and thought he had never seen any maiden so beautiful. While the dance went on, he slipped the gold ring onto her finger without her noticing it, and told the musicians to continue the dance.

When at last it ended, he tried to hold fast to the maiden's hand, but she tore herself away, and disappeared from sight. Allerleirauh ran back to her room, but she had stayed at the dance more than a half-hour. She didn't have time to take off her beautiful dress, but was obliged to throw her coat of skins over it. Neither did she quite finish the blackening of her skin, but left one finger white. Then she ran into the kitchen, cooked the soup for the King, and put the golden reel in it while the cook was upstairs.

When the King found the reel at the bottom of his soup dish, he summoned Allerleirauh. At once he noticed her one white finger, and the ring which he had put on it during the dance. He took her by the hand and held her fast. When she tried to run away, her cloak of skins fell back and the starry dress could be seen.

Then the King pulled the cloak off, and she could no longer conceal herself. The soot was washed from her face, and the whole court gasped at her beauty.

"You are my dear bride," the King said, "and we shall never be separated." The wedding was celebrated, and they lived happily all their lives.

Snow White and Rose Red

A WOMAN and her two daughters once lived on the edge of the forest. In their garden grew two rose bushes. One bore roses as red as blood and the other, roses white as the snow.

The widow's two daughters were much like the rose bushes. One was fair and the other dark; so their mother called them Snow White and Rose Red. They were both good children, but while Rose Red liked to run about the fields, Snow White preferred to stay at home with her mother.

The two girls were loved by everyone. The rabbits came to eat from their hands, and the deer would walk through the woods with them. If, by chance, the girls were caught in the forest at night, they were not afraid, for they knew nothing would hurt them.

One night, as they were returning home, darkness came. They lay down where they were and slept soundly. When they awoke in the morning, they saw a white-robed child standing beside them. He smiled and disappeared. They looked around and discovered that they had been lying at the very edge of a steep cliff. If they had gone a few steps farther, they would have crashed to their death on the rocks below. When they told their mother, she said the angel who cares for good children had watched over them.

Snow White and Rose Red kept their mother's house as clean and neat as a pin. In the evening the girls and their mother sat beside the fire, and often their mother read to them from a great book while the girls spun.

One snowy winter evening as they sat before the fire, a rap was heard at the door.

"Open the door, Rose Red," their mother said. "Some poor traveler has probably lost his way."

Rose Red opened the door, then jumped back, for there in the open doorway stood a huge black bear.

"Please, may I come in and lie by your fire?" he asked.

Rose Red hesitated, but her mother said, "Let him in, Rose Red. It is cold tonight and we shall share our fire with him."

The bear came in and lay down on the hearth. At first the girls were afraid of him, but he spoke kindly to them and they soon lost their fear.

"Will you please sweep some of the snow from my coat?" the bear asked.

Snow White got the broom and swept the snow from the big animal's coat. After that they became the best of friends. The bear slept beside the fire all night, and in the morning he left. But that night he rapped again at the door, and he was again allowed to lie beside the fire. And every night all that winter, the bear rapped at the door when darkness came and was let in. Snow White and Rose Red played with him and he growled pleasantly and would not think of hurting them.

One morning when the snow had disappeared from the ground and spring was on the way, the bear said, "Good-bye, I will not see you again this summer. I must go into the forest to live."

"But what will you do?" asked Snow White.

"I must look after my gold and jewels so that the dwarfs

do not steal them. In the winter my treasures are quite safe,
for when everything is frozen, the little men must stay
underground. But when spring comes again, they are up
on earth and I must watch them. If they get hold of any
treasure it is hard to get it back, for they hide it well." With
this the bear left.

Just as he was going, he caught his skin on the door and
tore it. Snow White declared she saw the glitter of gold
beneath his shaggy coat.

That summer the two girls missed their friend very much,
but they kept busy and happy. One day as they were going
into the forest to pick berries, they saw a tree that had been
blown down. Something strange was hopping about in the
branches. As they came closer, they saw that it was a little
dwarf who had caught his long white beard in a crack of
the tree.

"Here, you creatures!" the little man said crossly. "Can't
you see I'm caught? Why don't you get me out?"

The girls tried to help him. They pulled at the beard, but
it would not come loose. Then Rose Red remembered she
had some scissors in her pocket and she cut off the end of
the little fellow's beard.

The dwarf was now free, but he was not happy.

"Foolish creatures!" he complained crossly. "Why did
you cut my beard? Now my beautiful white beard is ruined."
And still muttering to himself, he picked up the bag of
gold that lay under the tree trunk and ran off into the forest
without so much as a thank you.

One day not long after this, Rose Red and Snow White
went to the river to fish. As they neared the bank, they saw
something hopping about like a great grasshopper. When
they reached the bank they saw it was the same dwarf they
had freed from the tree. This time he had been fishing and
his beard had become tangled in his line. A fish was caught

on the hook and was now pulling both line and dwarf away with him. The dwarf was struggling fiercely, but the fish was stronger than the little man.

Snow White and Rose Red hung on to the little man and tried to untangle the beard, but they could not. Rose Red again took out her scissors and cut the beard. The little man was now free from the line.

He picked up the bag of pearls that lay in the rushes, and without so much as a backward look, he went off into the forest, mumbling, "Stupid creatures! Look at my beard now! It is not enough to cut off the tip; now they have taken the best part of it."

Shortly after this, the girls were sent on an errand to the village. They had to go across an open field, and just as they reached the middle of it, an eagle swooped down and clutched at something in the grass. Whatever it was put up a fight for its life. As the girls drew near they saw that it was the same little dwarf again. They ran to his aid and held him until the eagle finally flew away.

When the little man had recovered from his fright, he said crossly, "Couldn't you have been more careful? You have let the eagle tear holes in my brown coat."

Frowning fiercely, the dwarf picked up a bag of jewels and disappeared in a hole beneath a rock. The girls were accustomed to his rudeness by this time, and they went on their way to town.

Returning the same way that evening, they came across the dwarf again. He was sitting on the ground with jewels all around him. The setting sun shone on the lovely gems and made them sparkle with such beautiful colors that the girls gasped in wonder.

"Why do you stand gaping there?" the dwarf shouted, and his face turned red with rage.

Just then a big black bear appeared out of the forest. The

dwarf sprang with terror toward his cave, but he was not quick enough. The bear caught the little man and hit him just once. He never moved again. Snow White and Rose Red were frightened and had started to run home, but the bear called to them, "Snow White, Rose Red, do not run away. I am your friend, the bear."

Snow White and Rose Red turned around and there, where the bear had stood, was a handsome Prince. The shaggy bearskin lay beside him.

"I was bewitched by the wicked dwarf and made to run about the forest as a bear," the Prince explained. "But now that the dwarf is dead, I am free again. All the gold and jewels that he had are mine, for he stole them from me."

The girls rejoiced with him that he was now in his true form again. The Prince invited them to come to his castle, and they went gladly and their mother with them.

In due time Snow White married the Prince, and Rose Red married his brother. They all lived happily together, and beside the palace door they planted the two rose bushes that had once bloomed beside their humble cottage. Every year one bore red, red roses and the other had roses as white as the snow.

The Old Woman in the Wood

A MAIDSERVANT was once traveling with her master's party when they were waylaid by robbers in the heart of a dense wood. Everyone was murdered except the servant girl, who jumped from the carriage and hid behind a tree. The robbers rode away in the coach and the poor girl was left alone.

As she sat down under a tree wondering what would become of her, a dove with a golden key in its mouth flew to her.

"In yonder tree there is a lock," the dove said. "Open it with this key and you will find something to eat."

The girl went to the tree and opened the little door. Inside on a shelf was a loaf of white bread and a pitcher of milk. The girl ate hungrily and, when she had finished, she said, "The birds of the air have nests, but I have no place to sleep."

The dove flew down to her with another key. "Open the next tree," he said.

The girl did as she was told and found there a comfortable bed. She lay down and slept till morning.

When morning came the dove brought a third key. "This will open the next tree," he said. "There you will find clothes to wear."

The girl opened the tree and found finer clothes than she had ever worn before.

For many days the girl lived like this, with the dove caring for all her wants. Then one day the dove said to her, "Will you do something for me?"

"I'll do anything you wish, for you have been very kind to me," the girl answered. "Tell me what you want."

"I will take you to a little house," said the dove. "Enter it and you will find an old woman sitting beside the fire. She will say good day to you, but you must not answer her. Go past her and open a door that leads into a room beyond. On the table and on the floor you will see heaps of rings. Pass by all the jeweled rings. Search until you find a plain gold band. Bring it to me as fast as you can."

The dove showed the girl the way to the little house in the wood. She opened the door and found a little old woman sitting before the fire just as the dove had said. The woman spoke, but the girl said nothing and went on to the door on the other side of the room.

"What are you doing here?" the old woman asked and tried to snatch at the girl's gown.

The girl brushed past her and went into the next room. There on the table and on the floor were piles and piles of beautiful rings. Some were gold and some were silver and all were set with precious stones. The girl looked carefully through each pile for a plain gold band.

The old woman had followed her, and now the girl noticed that she was trying to slip out carrying a bird cage. The girl whirled around and snatched the cage from the old woman. In it was a bird, and in the bird's bill was the plain gold band.

The girl reached into the cage and took the ring. Then she hurried out of the little house and through the wood until she came to the tree where the dove had been. Panting from her haste, she leaned against the tree to wait for her friend.

As she stood there, the tree seemed to grow softer. It seemed to lean down gently and wrap its branches about her. Astonished, the girl turned about and discovered that it was no longer a tree but a Prince, who took her in his arms and gently kissed her.

"You have released me from the power of the old woman," the Prince said. "She bewitched me and turned me into a tree, and a tree I had to remain, except for two hours a day when I was a dove. Only the plain gold ring could release me."

The Prince's servants and horses that had also been turned into trees were freed, too, and again took their natural forms. The Prince and the servant girl rode at once to his father's castle. There they were married and lived happily for many, many years.

Rapunzel

THERE WAS ONCE a man and his wife who were very lonely because they had no child. One day as the wife stood at her window she happened to glance over the wall into the neighboring garden and saw a bed of fine green rampion. It looked fresher and crisper than any rampion the woman had ever seen, and she longed to eat some.

"Ah, what a tasty salad that would make," she thought to herself. "How I wish I had some."

But there was no use wishing, for the garden belonged to a witch who never let anyone have a taste of what grew there.

Every day the woman looked at the rampion, and every day her desire to eat some grew stronger. Before long she could not look at the rampion without her mouth watering. No other food seemed good to her, and she pushed away her meals untouched and went up to gaze at the rampion. She became so weak and pale from lack of food that her husband despaired of her life. At length he determined to steal some rampion from the witch's garden, no matter what might befall.

That evening he climbed over the wall of the witch's garden, hastily snatched a handful of rampion, and brought it to his wife. She made it into a salad and gobbled it down greedily. This dish pleased her so much that she found

213

her desire for rampion three times as great as before. So nothing would do but that her husband must once more venture into the garden.

That evening at dusk the man boosted himself over the wall again, but without the good fortune he had had in his first venture. Just as he clutched the rampion in his hand, the witch appeared.

"How dare you come into my garden like a thief and steal my rampion?" she challenged him in a high shrill voice. "Evil shall befall you for this!"

"Alas!" replied the man. "Pray be merciful, for I have only come here in great need. My wife saw your rampion from the window and felt so strong a desire for it that she would have died if it had not been gratified."

"Ah," said the witch, rubbing her hands together greedily. "If you want it so much, you will pay me well for it, eh? I will give you the rampion as frequently as you please. But this is the price: you must give me your first child. Do not fear for the child's safety, as I will tend it as a mother."

The man, in his fright, promised what the witch asked. When his first child was born, the witch appeared immediately to claim it. She gave the baby the name of Rapunzel and took it away with her.

Rapunzel became the loveliest child that the sun ever shone upon. When she was twelve years old Rapunzel's beauty was so great that the jealous witch shut her up in a tower. There were neither steps nor door to the building, and only a very small window at the top. When the witch desired to enter, she stood beneath the window and cried, "Rapunzel! Rapunzel! Let down your hair."

Now Rapunzel had great quantities of hair, as bright and fine as gold. When she heard the witch's voice, she unbound her tresses and let them fall from the window. Climbing these, the old woman entered the tower.

After two or three years, it happened that the King's son passed by the tower while riding through the wood. He heard a voice singing so enchantingly that he was compelled to stop and listen. It was Rapunzel singing to while away the lonely hours in her tower.

In vain the Prince sought a door by which to enter the strange tower and reach the singer. Finding none, he returned home disconsolate. The voice had so deeply touched his heart that every day he rode to the wood to listen to it.

One day while he was standing behind a tree, he saw the witch approach and heard the words, "Rapunzel! Let down your hair." He saw the shining locks let down and the old woman climb to the tower.

"Ah! So that is the ladder by which they ascend," said the King's son. "I will try my luck, too."

The next day as it began to grow dark, he went to the tower and cried, "Rapunzel! Rapunzel! Let down your hair!" Instantly the hair fell down, and the Prince ascended.

Rapunzel shrank back with terror when she saw a man's head appear over her balcony wall, for she had never seen such a being before. The Prince spoke kindly to her and told her how her charming voice had touched his heart. Then he asked her to become his wife. Since he was young and handsome, Rapunzel said to herself, "He will certainly love me more than the old woman does." Therefore, she laid her hand on his and willingly consented.

She added, "I would gladly leave this place and follow you, but I do not know how to get down. You must bring a silken cord with you every time you come. I will twist it into a ladder, and when it is finished, I will descend. Then you shall take me away with you on your horse."

They agreed that until the ladder was ready the Prince should come to the tower every evening, as the old woman only came during the day. So it went on, and the witch discovered nothing of their meetings until one day, Rapunzel thoughtlessly said, "Good mother, how is it that you are so much heavier to draw up than the King's son? He takes but a moment to climb up to me."

"What do I hear, you wicked child?" screamed the old woman. "I thought I had shut you away from all the world, and yet you have deceived me."

In her anger she seized Rapunzel by the hair, grasped her scissors and—snip, snap—the long locks lay on the floor. Then she sent poor Rapunzel into a desert, and left her to wander about alone.

The evening of that same day, the witch bound Rapunzel's locks to a hook in the window. When the King's son came and cried, "Rapunzel! Rapunzel! Let down your hair," the witch let the shorn hair descend from above. The King's son mounted as usual, but at the top, instead of Rapunzel, he found the furious old witch.

"Eh!" she said with an evil laugh. "You have come for your sweetheart, but she is no longer here. Rapunzel is lost to you forever! You will never see her again!"

The King's son was beside himself with grief, and in his despair, he leaped from the tower. He escaped with his life, but the thorns among which he fell scratched out his eyes and he wandered blindly up and down the country.

Several miserable years passed, and at last his wanderings led him into the desert where Rapunzel was living. One day he heard her singing, and the remembered sweetness of her voice set his heart aflame. Calling her name, he stumbled toward her. Rapunzel instantly recognized her Prince and fell weeping on his neck. Two of her tears moistened his eyes, and instantly he could see.

With great joy they set out for the Prince's kingdom, where they were joyfully received and lived ever after in happiness and peace.

The Steadfast Tin Soldier

ONCE, LONG AGO, there were twenty-five soldiers who were all brothers because they had been made from the same old tin spoon. Each soldier stood very straight and wore a splendid uniform of red and blue.

The first thing they heard, as the lid was taken off their box, was a small boy clapping his hands and shouting, "Soldiers, soldiers!" He took each of them out of their box and stood them on the table with the rest of his birthday presents.

Now all these soldiers were exactly alike, with the exception of one who had only one leg. You see, he had been the last one made, and there wasn't quite enough tin to finish him. But he stood just as straight on his one leg as the others did on two, and he is the hero of this story.

There were many other toys on the table, but the one that caught everyone's eye was a beautiful little cardboard castle. You could see right into the bright rooms through the tiny windows, and the outside was surrounded by a glass lake with waxen swans swimming on it. Altogether it made a charming picture, but the prettiest thing of all was the lovely little lady who stood in the open door of the cardboard castle.

She also was made out of cardboard, and she wore a beautiful dress of light gauze. Over her shoulders was a

217

dainty blue ribbon with a brilliant spangle on one end of it. She stood with her arms outstretched, for she was a dancer and had kicked one foot so high in the air that the soldier supposed that she, like himself, had only one leg.

"She would be a fine wife for me," the soldier thought to himself, "but she is far too grand. She lives in a fine castle, and I live in a box which I share with twenty-four other soldiers. But I must, at least, try to speak to her." He stood behind a snuff box on the table, and from there he could watch the little lady who continued to pose daintily on her one pointed toe.

Later that evening the other tin soldiers were put away, and all the people of the house went to bed. Then the toys began to play. The tin soldiers rattled inside their box, because they could not get the lid off. The nutcracker turned somersaults. The pencil scribbled on the paper. The canary woke up and joined the fun by talking in verse. The only two who did not move were the tin soldier and the dancing lady. He stood very straight on his one leg, never taking his eyes off the little lady who stood so prettily with both arms outstretched.

As the clock struck twelve, the lid flew off the snuff box, and a little black goblin popped out.

"Tin soldier," he said, "take your eyes away from what does not concern you." But the soldier pretended that he didn't hear him. "You just wait until tomorrow," threatened the goblin.

The next morning when the children got up, they placed the tin soldier on the window sill. Whether it was the goblin or a puff of wind, I do not know, but the soldier fell head first out of the window. The maid and the little boy ran out to look for him and, although they almost stepped right on him, they could not see him. The soldier had only to call out and say, "Here I am," but he did not feel that it was proper for him to shout when he was in uniform.

After a while it began to rain, first a spattering and then by the bucketful, a regular cloudburst. When the storm was over, two little boys came running by.

"Look here!" cried one of them. "It's a tin soldier! Let's send him sailing." They made a boat out of a newspaper, put the soldier in the middle of it, and sailed it down the gutter, while they ran alongside clapping their hands. The paper boat rolled and rocked and sometimes swirled around, but the soldier continued to stand steadfastly at his post. Suddenly, the boat went into a dark tunnel.

"Where am I going now?" he wondered. "If only the little lady were with me, I would not care. This is all the little black goblin's fault."

As these thoughts ran through his head, a big water rat appeared, shouting, "Have you got a passport? Give me your passport." The soldier didn't say a word, but kept his eyes straight ahead. The rat raced after the boat, calling all the way, "Hold him! Hold him! He hasn't paid a toll—he hasn't shown his passport!"

The current grew stronger and stronger, and the tin soldier could see daylight ahead. But he could also hear a great roar ahead, for the drain ended in a canal. To the little tin soldier that was as dangerous as going over a waterfall. The boat rushed out into the canal, and the soldier stiffened himself while the boat swirled around.

Finally it became filled with water. The paper grew limp and collapsed, and as the water closed over his head, the soldier thought of the little dancer and how he would never see her again. At just that moment a big fish came along and swallowed him.

It was *so* dark inside of the fish, even darker than it had been in the tunnel. The fish swam to and fro, then suddenly was snatched away. It bumped about and then lay very still.

Finally light appeared. The soldier heard someone say, "A tin soldier!"

The fish had been caught, sold in the market, and brought into the kitchen where the cook had cut it open with a large knife. She picked up the soldier and carried him into the parlor where everyone was exclaiming over the wonderful man who traveled around in the stomach of a fish.

But the tin soldier scarcely listened. When they set him on the table, he saw that by some wonderful miracle he was back in the same room that he had been in before. The same children and the same toys were there, and best of all the beautiful little castle with the little dancing lady standing in front of it. She was still balancing herself on one leg, and when the tin soldier saw how faithful she had been, he almost wept tin tears.

At this very moment, one of the boys picked up the soldier and flung him into the fire. He had no reason for doing this, so it must have been the fault of the goblin. The heat became unbearable, and the soldier's gay colors ran together in a sorry blue. Still he stood there, steadfast and sturdy, and continued to gaze tenderly at the little lady.

Then suddenly a door opened; a draft of air caught up the dancer. She fluttered straight into the fire beside the soldier, blazed up in bright glory, and was gone. By this time the soldier had melted down to a lump, and when the maid cleaned out the fireplace the next morning, she found him in the shape of a little tin heart.

All that was left of the dancer was her spangle, and that had been burned as black as coal.

The Miller Boy and the Cat

THERE WAS ONCE a miller who had neither wife nor children.

But he did have three apprentice boys who worked for him. The miller was growing old and wished to leave the mill to one of his apprentices. In order to discover which lad would be the best, he determined to test them.

"Go out into the world," he said to them one day, "and bring back a horse. The boy who brings the finest horse shall have the mill."

The three boys started out together. They walked all day and that night lay down in a cave to sleep. When the two oldest boys were sure the youngest was sound asleep, they quietly stole away, for they did not wish to have him tagging along after them.

When the youngest boy woke in the morning, he found he was alone.

"How can I ever find a horse alone?" he thought. Not knowing what else to do, he walked on into the wood.

"What are you doing here, Hans?" asked a voice near him.

Hans, surprised to hear someone calling him by name, looked around and saw a small black and white cat.

"You cannot help me," Hans said.

"I know what you want," the cat said. "You are looking

for a horse. If you come and work for me seven years, I will give you a horse."

The miller's boy was surprised at this offer but decided to accept it and see what would happen. Away they went through the wood to the cat's home. They entered a fine house and the miller's boy was served all sorts of good food. All the servants were kittens. They whisked up and down the stairs and all about the house, keeping it as neat as a pin. When evening came they played on many different instruments to while away the hours until bedtime. At length the kittens led the miller boy to his room and helped him take off his clothes. Then they blew out the light and scampered away.

In the morning the kittens were on hand again to help him dress. After breakfast, the cat gave Hans an ax, a wedge, a saw of silver, and a mallet of copper, and told him to cut wood into little pieces for her. Day after day Hans went on cutting wood and seeing no one but the black and white cat and the energetic kittens.

One day the cat gave Hans a silver scythe and a gold whetstone and said, "Go and mow the meadow and spread the grass to dry."

Hans did that and everything else that the cat requested. He began to think that it was almost time for the cat to give him his horse. One day he asked the cat about it.

"There is one more thing I want you to do," she said. "Build me a little house. When it is finished you may have your horse."

Hans worked hard at the house, and in what seemed a short time it was done.

"Come with me," said the cat. "I will show you your horse." She took him to the stables where there were twelve horses, each one as beautiful as the next. She watered them and fed them and then said to Hans, "You may go home

now, and in three days your horse will come to you."

Hans started for home. He had nothing to show for all the seven years of labor, not even a new suit of clothes. When he reached the mill he found that the two older apprentices were there ahead of him. One had brought back a lame horse, and the other a poor beast blind in both eyes.

When they saw Hans coming empty-handed, they laughed and called out, "Where is your horse?"

"It will be here tomorrow," Hans replied. But he didn't speak very firmly, for he was beginning to wonder about it.

"Ha! Ha! He! He!" tittered the older lads. "A horse that drives itself home. That is a fine one surely."

Hans made no answer and went on to the mill. The miller would not let so shabby a boy into his clean mill, and poor Hans had to sleep that night in the shed where the geese were kept.

Early the next morning a fine coach drew up to the door of the mill. A lovely Princess opened the door and stepped out. She went straight to the mill and asked for Hans.

"He was so ragged and dirty," the miller said, "that we could not have him in the mill. He slept in the shed with the geese last night."

"Give him these boxes," the Princess commanded, "and then bring him to me." The miller obeyed and soon discovered that the boxes contained a velvet coat, a plumed hat and other princely garments.

While Hans was dressing himself, the Princess asked to see the horses the other miller boys had brought. They showed her the two sorry nags, one lame and the other blind. Then a servant led in a splendid horse and told the miller that Hans had earned it. The miller had to admit that this was the finest horse that had been in his yard for many a day.

Just then Hans appeared in his new clothes, and no Prince could have looked finer.

"Hans, Hans, look at me," said the Princess. "I am the cat you served faithfully for seven years."

But Hans could only stare in love and wonder at her beauty.

"Hans, Hans!" the miller said. "The mill is yours, for you have brought the finest horse."

"No," said the Princess, "you may keep the horse and the mill, for Hans is going with me."

She took Hans by the hand and led him to the coach. They got in and rode away. When they came to the place where Hans had built the little house, a beautiful castle stood in its place. The Princess and Hans were married there, and they were both wealthy and happy and never wanted for anything.

The Six Swans

THERE WAS ONCE a King who was forced by trickery to choose for his second wife a woman who was the daughter of a witch. However, the King was wise enough to hide his seven children from their stepmother, for he knew that she would harm them if she could.

He took them to a lonely castle which stood in the midst of a forest so thick that no one could get through it without the aid of magic. A wise woman had shown the King this enchanted castle and had told him how to reach it. When the King threw a ball of magic yarn before him it would unwind of itself and lead the way through the forest to the castle. In this way he could visit his children as often as he liked. He felt sure that they would always be safe.

One day the stepmother heard the servants talking about the King's six young sons, and she determined in her evil heart to find them and get rid of them. She had learned something of magic from her witch mother, and so she used this power to make six little shirts which would cast an evil spell on whoever wore them.

She kept both ears open and her tongue quiet and soon learned about the magic ball of yarn. The next time the King was away, the wicked Queen took the yarn and with it found the way to the enchanted castle. The six young Princes came running to meet her, for they thought she was

their father. Before they could turn and run she thre
magic shirts over their heads. Instantly the six boys
turned into swans and flew up over the forest and away.

The Queen went home well pleased with her evil trick,
but she did not know that the seventh child, a beautiful
young girl, had remained in the castle and had seen the
whole thing.

"Alas!" sighed the maiden. "How can I bear to stay here
in the castle without my brothers? I shall go into the world
and rest neither day nor night until I find them."

So she started out, keeping her eyes ever on the sky in
hope of seeing the six swans. She walked all that day, all
that night, and all the next day. At length she could keep
her eyes open no longer and knew that she must find a place
to rest.

Just as she thought she could not go a step farther, she
spied a small brown hut on the edge of a marshy stream.
There was no one in the hut, but six beds, neatly made with
white spreads and ruffled pillows, stood against the wall.
She did not dare lie down on the beds for fear of annoying
the owners, but she curled up on a rug in the corner and
soon was sound asleep.

Presently she was awakened by a strange rustling noise.
She opened her eyes wide in amazement as six beautiful
white swans swooped in through the open window.

Before the maiden could cry out, the six swans formed a
circle and began blowing at each other. The white swan
feathers blew off and vanished, the skins came off like shirts,
and out stepped the six brothers. The maiden rushed to
them, trying to kiss all six at once.

At last the eldest brother stopped the glad celebration,
saying, "Our joy has a short life, little sister. We are our
own selves for a quarter of an hour each evening. The rest
of the time we are swans."

The maiden was sober for a moment, and then said
firmly, "A quarter of an hour is better than nothing. I shall
stay here and wait each evening for your coming."

The eldest brother shook his head sadly.

"No, no, little sister. This hut belongs to a band of
wicked robbers. When they come home and find you, they
will kill you at once."

But the maiden would not be daunted.

"Surely there is a way to break the wicked spell," she
said.

"Yes, we have already learned it," answered her brother.
"But alas, it is too difficult for any human being to accomplish. For six years you must neither speak nor laugh, and
in that time you must make a shirt for each of us. You must
make the thread yourself out of nettles. From this moment
on, if a single word falls from your lips, we shall evermore
be swans."

The maiden pressed her lips together firmly.

"What *must* be done, *can* be done," she thought to herself.

At this very instant the quarter of an hour was finished,
and the brothers became swans and flew off over the marsh.
The maiden went at once to gather nettles, and although
the rough leaves stung her dainty hands till they were red
and blistered, she said not a word but kept at it until she
had made the nettles into thread. Then she built herself a
hut of sticks in the top of a huge oak tree and lived there
like the squirrels. She neither spoke nor laughed but kept
steadily at her work.

One day the King of a nearby country came hunting
through the forest. His huntsmen spied the maiden and
called to her to come down. The King also beseeched her
to descend, for he had fallen in love with her at sight.

The maiden did not answer, but the King would not be

discouraged. He boldly asked her to be his bride. The maiden said no word, but she nodded her head. The King leaped from his horse and climbed the tree and fetched the maiden down. She came with him willingly, and brought with her a great bundle of nettles. Joyfully the King placed the beautiful girl on the saddle before him and hastened home. The wedding was celebrated with feasting and merry-making and through it all the bride said never a word.

The King soon grew used to her silence and was happy and contented with his sweet, gentle bride. He let her knit all day long and brought her soothing oils to heal the blisters made by the sharp nettles.

All would have gone well if it had not been for the King's jealous stepmother who had been used to having her own way at court before the young Queen came. When the young Queen's baby was born, this jealous stepmother stole it from the cradle and told the King that his wife had destroyed it. Since the Queen would not speak to defend herself, the King had to believe his stepmother. The poor young Queen was condemned as a witch and ordered to be burned alive.

A great fire was kindled in the courtyard, and the Queen was led forth, still knitting on the last of the six shirts, with the other five in a bag at her belt, for it was the last day of the six years. Only one sleeve of the last shirt remained unfinished. The Queen was bound to the stake, and the red flames began to lick her clothing.

Just then the air was filled with a great rustling of wings, and six beautiful white swans dropped from the sky and flew about the Queen in graceful circling flight. As each bird passed before her she threw a shirt over its head. Instantly the birds became six handsome youths who leaped upon the flames and stamped them to ashes. But the youngest of the six had one arm only; the other was still a swan's wing because of the unfinished sleeve.

Now at last the young Queen could speak and tell her husband the truth. The jealous stepmother was forced to bring back the baby which she had stolen, and the whole palace was filled with great rejoicing. The jealous stepmother was so angry that she went into a fit and died, but the King and the Queen and her six brothers lived in happiness and peace.

Hans in Luck

HANS HAD SERVED his master for seven years, and at the end of that time Hans said, "Master, the time I pledged to serve you is up. I should like to go home to my mother. Please may I have my wages?"

His master replied, "You have served me faithfully and honestly, Hans, for seven long years, and as your service was, so shall be your reward."

With these words, he gave Hans a lump of gold as big as his head. Hans took his handkerchief from his pocket, wrapped the gold in it, swung it over his shoulder and set out on the road toward his home village. The big lump of gold bumped and thumped against his shoulder and he began to wish it were not so heavy.

As he walked along, a horseman came in sight. He trotted along gaily on a fine animal.

"Ah!" said Hans, aloud. "What a fine thing riding is! That one is seated, as it were, upon a chair, while I must walk in the dust lugging this lump of gold."

The rider, overhearing the word "gold" and recognizing Hans as a foolish fellow, said slyly, "If you like, we can exchange. I will give you my horse, and you can give me your lump of gold."

"With all my heart," cried Hans. "But I will tell you fairly you are undertaking a heavy burden."

The man dismounted before Hans could change his mind, took the gold, and helped Hans onto the horse. Giving him the reins, he said, "Now, when you want to go faster, just cluck with your tongue and cry, 'Gee up! Gee up!' "

Hans was delighted when he found himself on the horse, riding along so gaily with no burden to carry. After a while he thought he should like to go faster. So he cried, "Gee up! Gee up!" as the man had told him. Off went the horse at a hard trot, and before Hans knew what he was about, he was thrown head over heels into a ditch.

The horse would have run off if he had not been stopped by a peasant who came along just then, driving a cow before him. Hans picked himself up, shook his fist at the horse, and said angrily, "I will never ride that animal again! Who could want such a prankish nag? Owning a cow is much more sensible. With a cow you can have milk, butter and cheese every day. Ah! What I wouldn't give for a cow!"

"Well," said the peasant, "I will exchange my cow for your prankish horse."

Hans was delighted at the bargain, and so was the peasant. He quickly gave Hans the cow and, swinging himself upon the horse, rode off in a hurry.

Now Hans drove his cow steadily before him.

As soon as he came to an inn, he halted, and with great satisfaction ate all the lunch he had brought with him. After this he again drove his cow along the road in the direction of his mother's village. As the day grew hotter and hotter, Hans became very thirsty.

"This will never do," he thought. "I will milk my cow and refresh myself." He tied her to a tree and, having no pail, placed his cap below. But try as he would, he could not get a drop of milk. The impatient cow gave him such a

kick on the head that he tumbled to the ground. Hans lay
in the dirt, holding his head and moaning.

Soon a butcher came along pushing a wheelbarrow in
which there was a young pig.

"What on earth has happened?" he exclaimed, helping
poor Hans to his feet; and Hans told him all that had occurred.
The butcher then said, "Your cow will never give any
milk. She is an old beast, and is only good for the butcher!"

"Oh! Oh!" said Hans, pulling his hair over his eyes.
"Who would have thought it? I have no desire for cow's
meat; it is too tough. Now a young pig like yours tastes like
something!"

"Well, now," said the butcher, "I will make an exchange
and let you have my pig for your cow."

"Heaven reward you for your kindness!" cried Hans and,
giving up the cow, he untied the pig from the wheelbarrow.

Hans walked on again, pleased that everything had happened just as he wished. Presently a boy overtook him, carrying a fine white goose under his arm.

"Good day," said the boy.

"Good day to you," said Hans, and he began to talk
about his luck and about what profitable exchanges he
had made.

The boy told him that he was carrying the goose to a
christening feast.

"Just feel how heavy it is," the boy said. "Why, it has
been fattened for eight weeks. Whoever gets a bite of this
will have to wipe the grease from each side of his mouth!"

"Yes," said Hans, holding it with one hand. "It is
heavy, but my pig is no trifle either."

While he was speaking, the boy kept looking about on all
sides and shaking his head suspiciously. At length he broke
out, "I wouldn't say much about that pig if I were you. A
pig has just been stolen from the mayor, and I am afraid

it is that very same pig under your arm. It will be bad for you if anyone catches you."

Honest Hans was thunderstruck, and he exclaimed, "Ah, Heaven help me in this new trouble! You know the neighborhood better than I do and can hide. You take my pig and let me have your goose."

"That will be a risk," replied the boy, "but still I do not wish to be the cause of your having any misfortune." Quickly he drove the pig off by a side path, while Hans walked on toward home with the goose under his arm.

As he came to the last village on his road home, Hans met a knife-grinder seated beside a hedge, whirling his wheel round and singing:

> "Scissors and razors and knives I grind;
> A sharper fellow is hard to find."

Hans stopped to watch a bit and said, "You appear to have a very good business here, if I may judge by your merry song."

"Yes," answered the grinder. "A true knife-grinder is a man who always has money in his pocket. But what a fine goose you have. Where did you buy it?"

"I did not buy it at all," said Hans, "but took it in exchange for my pig."

"And where did you get the pig?"

"I exchanged it for my cow, which I exchanged for a horse."

"And the horse?"

"I gave a lump of gold as big as my head for him."

"And the gold?"

"That was my wages for seven years' work."

"I see you have bettered yourself each time you have traded," said the grinder. "But now if you could hear money rattling in your pocket as you walked, your fortune would surely be made."

"Well, how shall I manage that?" asked Hans.

"You must become a grinder like me. In this trade you need nothing but a grindstone. I will give you a stone for your goose. Are you agreeable?"

"How can you ask me?" said Hans. "Why, I shall be the luckiest man in the world."

"Now," said the grinder, picking up an ordinary stone which lay nearby. "There you have a fine stone. Take it, and use it very carefully!"

Hans took the stone and, giving the grinder the goose, walked on with a satisfied air.

"I must have been born to a heap of luck," he thought. "Everything happens just as I wish."

Soon, however, he began to feel very tired, and very hungry, too, for he had been on his way since daybreak. At last he felt unable to go any farther with the heavy stone. He sighed deeply and thought what a good thing it would be if he no longer had to carry it.

Just then he noticed a stream flowing nearby. He decided to sit down beside it to rest and refresh himself. He carefully put the stone down and leaned over to scoop up some water in his hand. He pushed the stone a little too far and over it went into the stream with a loud splash. As it sank beneath the water Hans jumped up and clicked his heels for joy. Then he gave thanks that without even trying he had been delivered from his burden.

"There is no other man under the sun as lucky as I am," exclaimed Hans.

And with a light heart he went gaily along until he reached his mother's house.

Bearskin

THERE WAS ONCE a soldier who fought well and bravely, But when peace came and he received his discharge, he knew not where to go. His parents were dead and he had no home of his own; so he asked his brothers to take him in until he might find work to do.

But the brothers had hard hearts and answered that they could do nothing for him. The poor fellow had nothing in the world but his gun, so he shouldered it and went into the world.

He had not gone far when he came to a meadow in the middle of which stood a circle of trees. He sat down in the shade and thought gloomily of his fate.

"I have no money, no trade but war, and I am not fit for anything. I fear I shall have to die of hunger."

Just then he heard a noise and, lifting his eyes, he saw before him a stranger, handsomely dressed in green, but with a hideous cloven hoof.

"I know what you want," said the stranger. "It is money. You shall have as much as you can carry. But first I want to convince myself that you are not afraid, for I give nothing to cowards."

"Soldier and coward," said the young man, "are two words that do not go together. You may put me to the test."

"Well, then," replied the stranger, "look behind you."

The soldier, turning around, saw a huge bear coming toward him, growling fiercely.

"Uh-oh," he said. "I'll tickle your nose for you and cure you of growling." He leveled his musket and shot the bear dead on the spot.

"I see," said the stranger, "that you do not lack courage, but there are other conditions you will have to fulfill."

"Nothing shall stop me," said the soldier, who saw he had to do with an evil spirit, "so long as my soul is not in danger."

"You shall judge for yourself," replied the spirit. "For seven years you are not to wash yourself, nor comb your hair, nor cut your nails. I will give you a coat and a cloak which you must wear during the whole time. If you die in the meantime, you'll belong to me. If you live longer than seven years, you shall be free and rich all your life."

The soldier thought of the poverty to which he was reduced. As he had so often defied death, he decided to face it once more, and accepted the proposal. The evil spirit took off his own coat and gave it to the soldier, saying, "So long as you wear this coat, whenever you put your hand into the pocket, you will bring out a handful of money." Then, having stripped the bear of its skin, he added, "This will serve you as a cloak and a bed as well, for you may have no other. Because of this clothing, you will be called 'Bearskin.'" Then the spirit vanished.

The soldier put on the coat and, thrusting his hand into his pocket, found that the stranger had not deceived him. He put the bearskin on his back and began to roam through the world, denying himself none of the good things which make people fat and their purses lean.

The first year his appearance was passable enough, but the second year he looked frightful. His hair almost completely covered his face, his beard was matted like a piece of felt, and his face was so entirely covered with dirt that if grass seed had been sown in it, he would have had a fine lawn. Everyone fled from him in terror. He gave to all the poor, begging them to pray that he might not die within seven years.

During the fourth year, he came to an inn where the owner refused to have him even in the stable for fear he would frighten the horses. But Bearskin drew a handful of gold from his pocket. The innkeeper changed his mind at the sight of it and gave him a room in the back of the house on condition that he would not let himself be seen and thus destroy the reputation of the establishment.

One evening Bearskin was sitting in his room wishing with all his heart that the seven years were over, when he heard someone sobbing in the next chamber. Being a good-hearted fellow, he opened the door and saw an old man with his head resting on his hands, shaking with sobs. When the old man saw Bearskin come in, he leaped up in fright and started to run away, but he grew calmer when he heard himself addressed by a human voice.

At last, by means of friendly words, Bearskin succeeded in persuading the old man to tell the cause of his sorrow. The old man said he had lost all his fortune and that he and his daughters were reduced to such poverty that he could not pay his bill and was going to be sent to prison.

"If that is the only cause of your grief," said Bearskin, "I've money enough for you." He summoned the innkeeper, paid him, and gave the old man a large sum besides.

The old man did not know how to express his gratitude.

"Come with me," he said. "My daughters are all beautiful; you shall choose one of them for your wife. She will not refuse when she hears what you have done for me."

Bearskin agreed to accompany the old man, but when the eldest daughter caught sight of the horrible-looking fellow,

she fled away with loud cries. The second stood her ground and looked over her suitor from head to foot. Then she flounced out, saying, "How am I to accept a husband who does not have a human face? I'd rather have the dancing bear I saw at the fair last week."

But the youngest daughter said, "Dear father, he must be a good man because he helped us. You have promised him a wife, and you must keep your word."

Unfortunately, Bearskin's face was covered with hair and dirt, or the daughter would have seen the flush of joy that spread over his cheeks as he heard these words. He took a ring from his finger, broke it in two, and gave one half to his betrothed bride. He begged her to keep it carefully, while he kept the other half.

On the piece he gave to her he wrote his own name, and on his piece he wrote her name. Then he left her, saying, "I must leave you for three years. If I come back we will be married, but if I do not come back, you will know I am dead, and you will be free. Pray that my life may be spared."

The poor betrothed maiden was sad, and the tears came into her eyes when she thought of her future husband.

As for the man with the bearskin, he wandered through the world, doing good whenever he was able and giving generously to the poor.

At last, when the last day of the seven years had come, he returned to the meadow and entered the circle of trees. A wind sprang up and the angry spirit appeared. He threw the soldier his old clothes and asked to have his own green coat back again.

"Wait a minute," said Bearskin. "First you must wash me, comb my hair, and cut my nails."

The evil spirit was obliged, very much against his will, to do as Bearskin commanded. The soldier now looked handsomer than he had at the beginning of the seven years.

Bearskin felt a great weight taken from his heart when the evil spirit departed without further tormenting him. He returned to the town, put on a magnificent velvet coat and, stepping into a carriage drawn by four white horses, drove to the house of his bride.

No one recognized him. The girls' father took him for an officer of high rank, and invited him into the room where his daughters sat. They put a delicious feast before him and declared they had never seen a more handsome cavalier. As to his betrothed, she sat opposite him in her black dress, with her eyes cast down, and said not a word.

At length the father asked him if he would marry one of his daughters. The two elder girls ran to their room to bedeck themselves with jewels and fine clothes, for each thought she would be the one chosen.

The stranger, left alone with his betrothed, took his half of the ring from his pocket and dropped it into a glass of wine which he offered her. When she had drunk the wine and seen the ring in the bottom of the glass, her heart beat quickly. She seized the other half which hung about her neck, and fitted the pieces together.

Then he said to her, "I am your bridegroom, whom you saw under a bear's skin. Now, by Heaven's mercy, I have recovered my own shape."

He took her in his arms and kissed her again and again. At this moment the two sisters came back, dressed in their finest clothes. When they saw that the handsome young man was for their sister, and that he was the man who had worn the bearskin, they stamped their feet in a pout and ran off.

But the soldier and the youngest daughter were married without delay, and they lived happily many, many years.

The Real Princess

ONCE UPON A TIME there was a Prince who wished to marry a Princess, but she had to be a *real* Princess. He traveled up and down the whole world trying to find one. He met plenty of Princesses, but he could never quite satisfy himself that any one of them was a *real* Princess.

Finally the Prince returned home sad at heart, for he wished very much to marry a real Princess.

One night a terrific storm came up. Thunder rolled and lightning flashed and the rain poured down in torrents. At the height of the storm, there was a knocking at the gate of the castle, and the old King went to open it.

A maiden stood outside the gate, and what a state she was in! The water ran from her hair and clothes. It dripped in at the heels of her shoes and dribbled out at the toes, but she said that she was a real Princess.

"Well, we shall soon find out about that," thought the old Queen as she went off to prepare the bedroom. Taking all the things off the bed, she laid a small pea upon the slats, and upon this she heaped twenty mattresses and twenty eiderdown quilts. When all was ready, she called the Princess, who was to sleep there that night.

In the morning the Queen asked the Princess how she had rested.

"Oh, wretchedly!" she answered. "Simply abominably! I

scarcely closed my eyes the whole night. Heaven knows what might have been in the bed, but I lay upon something hard, so that my whole body is black and blue. It was really dreadful."

Since she had felt the pea through the twenty mattresses and the twenty eiderdown quilts, it was evident that she was a real Princess, for no one but a real Princess could have had such a fine sense of feeling.

So the Prince married her, because now he knew that he had found a real Princess, and the pea was placed in the royal museum, where it may still be seen if no one has taken it away.

Cherry the Frog Bride

THERE WAS ONCE an old woman who had an only daughter called Cherry, because she liked cherries better than any other kind of food. Now Cherry's mother had no garden, and no money to buy cherries for her daughter. The only way she could get the fruit was to go to a neighboring nunnery and beg some from the nuns.

She dared not let her daughter go out by herself, as she was so very beautiful that the first man who saw her would surely carry her off. Now it happened that the abbess in charge of the nunnery was as fond of cherries as the girl. When the abbess found that much of her fine fruit was going to Cherry she was very angry and promised herself to make trouble for the girl the next chance she got.

One day three wandering Princes came to the town where Cherry and her mother lived and saw the fair maiden standing at the window, combing her beautiful long hair. Each of the three Princes fell deeply in love with her at sight.

"That girl shall be my bride," said the three, all in one voice. And then, turning on each other in jealous anger, they began to fight for the beautiful unknown maiden. The abbess, hearing the uproar, came to the gate.

On learning that Cherry was the cause of the battle, her old anger against the girl broke forth. In a fit of rage the abbess wished Cherry to be turned into an ugly frog that would sit under the bridge at the end of the world. The abbess had no sooner uttered this wish than poor Cherry became a frog and vanished. Now the three Princes had nothing to fight for, so, sheathing their swords again they went on toward their father's home.

Meanwhile, their father the King had grown old and illfitted for the business of reigning. He thought of giving up his kingdom, but could not decide to which son it should go. This was a point that his fatherly heart could not settle, for he loved all his sons alike.

"My dear children," he said, "I am growing old and should like to give up my kingdom, but I do not know which of you to choose for my heir, for I love all three of you. Besides, I wish to give the cleverest and best one of you to my people for their King. I have decided to give you three trials, and the one who accomplishes all three shall have the kingdom. The first task is to find one hundred yards of cloth so fine that I can draw it through my golden ring."

The Princes promised to do their best, and they all set out on the search.

The two eldest brothers took many coaches and servants to bring home the beautiful material but the youngest went off on foot. The three started off together, but soon came to a place where the roads branched off into several lanes. Two roads ran through smiling meadows with smooth paths and shady groves, but the third looked dreary and barren.

The two eldest brothers chose the pleasant ways, but the youngest turned and went whistling alone down the dreary road. The elder brothers bought all the fine pieces of cloth they saw, and soon their coaches and horses were bent under their burdens. The youngest Prince, on the other hand, journeyed on for many a day, but he found no place to buy even one yard of cloth. His heart sank, and with every mile he grew more and more sorrowful.

At last he came to a bridge and there he sat down to rest and sigh over his bad luck. An ugly-looking frog popped its head out of the water and asked what was troubling him.

The Prince said sharply, "Silly frog, you cannot help me."

"Who told you so?" said the frog. "Tell me what ails you."

After a while the Prince told the story.

"I will help you," said the frog.

It jumped into the stream and soon returned, dragging a small piece of linen. It was no bigger than one's hand, and by no means the cleanest cloth in the world. However, there it was, and the Prince was told to take it with him. He didn't want such a dirty-looking cloth, but still there was something in the frog's voice that pleased him, and he thought to himself, "It is better than nothing."

So he picked it up, put it in his pocket, thanked the frog and started for home. The farther the Prince went the heavier his pocket grew.

He trudged into the courtyard about the same time his brothers came dashing up with their horses and coaches all heavily laden. The old King was very glad to see his children, and pulled off his ring to determine who had done the best. In all the stock which the two eldest had brought, there was not one piece a tenth part of which would go through the ring.

The youngest brother reached into his pocket and, much to his surprise, out came a piece of soft, white cloth a thousand times more beautiful than anything the brothers had seen. It was so fine that it passed with ease through the ring. Indeed, two such pieces would readily have gone in together.

The King embraced the lucky youth, told his servants to throw the coarse linen into the sea, and said to his children, "Now you must set out on the second task I have set for you.

Bring me a little dog, so small that it will lie in a nutshell."

The three Princes were more than a little frightened to attempt such a task, but, as they all longed for the crown, they set out on their travels. At the crossroads they parted again. The youngest chose his old dreary road, while his brothers chose the fine smooth roads. The youngest Prince went on, finding not even one dog, until he came to the bridge.

He had scarcely seated himself when his old friend, the frog, sat down beside him and croaked, "What is the matter?"

This time the Prince had no doubt of the frog's power, and therefore told what he wanted.

"It shall be done for you," said the frog. Diving into the stream, it soon returned with a hazelnut, laid it at the Prince's feet, and told him to take it home with him. The Prince picked up the nut and went his way, well pleased.

This time the brothers had reached home before him and had brought with them many pretty little dogs. The old King, willing to help them all he could, sent for a large walnut shell and tried to put each little dog into it. One stuck fast with the hind foot out, another's head would not go in, a third one's forefoot hung out, and a fourth could not get its tail into the shell. In short, none was able to sit in this new kind of kennel.

When the dogs had been tried, the youngest Prince made his father a dutiful bow and gave him the hazelnut, begging him to crack it very carefully. The moment that this was done, a beautiful little dog ran out upon the King's hand, wagged its tail, fondled its new master, and, to the delight of the whole court, turned about and barked at the other little beasts in the most graceful manner.

The joy of everyone was great and the old King again embraced his lucky son, told his people to drown all the other dogs in the sea, and said to his children, "Dear sons, your weightiest tasks are now over. Listen to my last wish. Whoever brings home the fairest lady will have my throne."

The prize was so tempting that the Princes wasted no time in setting to work, each in his own way. The youngest was not in as good spirits as he had been the last time. He thought to himself, "The old frog has been able to do a great deal, but all its power can do nothing for me now. Where would it find a fair maiden for me, better still a fairer maiden than has ever been seen at my father's court?"

Meanwhile, he went on, and sighed with a heavy heart as he sat down beside the bridge.

"Ah, Frog," he said, "this time you can do me no good."

"Never mind," croaked the frog. "Only tell me what is the matter now."

Then the Prince told his old friend his trouble.

"Start back home," said the frog. "The fair maiden will follow, but take care not to laugh at whatever may happen." Then, as before, it sprang into the water and out of sight.

The Prince sighed. This time he had little trust in the frog's word. However, he started for home. He had not gone far when he heard a noise behind him and, looking around, he saw six large water rats dragging a large pumpkin as if it were a coach. On the box sat an old toad as coachman; behind sat two little tadpoles as footmen. Within the coach sat his friend the frog, rather ugly, but with something of a graceful air.

The Prince was so lost in his own thought that he scarcely looked at the coach, much less laughed at it.

The coach passed on and soon turned a corner and was hidden from sight. The Prince was astonished on turning the corner himself to find a handsome coach and six black horses standing there, with a coachman in gay livery. Within the coach sat the most beautiful lady he had ever seen. He recognized her at once as the fair Cherry whom he had loved.

As he came up, the servants opened the coach door and he was invited to seat himself beside the beautiful lady.

They soon came to his father's city, where his brothers with trains of fair ladies had already assembled. As soon as Cherry was seen, all the court gave her the crown of beauty. The delighted father embraced his youngest son, named him heir to the crown, and ordered all the other ladies sent away.

Then the youngest Prince married Cherry and lived long and happily with her, and indeed lives with her still if he is not dead.

Rumpelstiltskin

IN A CERTAIN KINGDOM, there once lived a poor miller who had a very beautiful daughter. She was shrewd and clever, and the miller was so vain and proud of her that he told the King of the land that his daughter could spin gold from straw.

Now this King was very fond of money, and when he heard the miller's boast, he ordered the girl to be brought before him. Then he led her to a room filled with straw, gave her a spinning wheel, and said, "All this must be spun into gold before morning, or you forfeit your life." In vain the poor maiden declared that she could do no such thing. The door was locked.

She sat down and began to weep over her hard fate. Suddenly the door opened, and a droll little man hobbled in.

"Good day to you, my good lass. Why are you weeping?" he asked her.

"Alas!" she answered. "I must spin this straw into gold, and I do not know how."

"What will you give me," asked the little man, "to do it for you?"

"My necklace," replied the maiden.

The little man took her at her word and set himself down to the wheel. Round and round it went, merrily, merrily, and presently all the straw was spun into gold.

When the King came and saw the gold, he was greatly pleased, but his heart grew still more greedy, and he again shut the miller's daughter in a room with a larger pile of straw. She did not know what to do, so she sat down and began to weep again.

Presently the same little man opened the door and said, "What will you give me to do your task?"

"The ring on my finger," the maiden replied.

So her little friend took the ring and began to work at the wheel. By morning all the straw was spun into gold.

The King was delighted to see all this glittering treasure, but still he was not satisfied. He took the miller's daughter into a still larger room filled with straw and said, "If all this is spun into gold before morning, you shall be my Queen."

As soon as the girl was alone the dwarf came in.

"What will you give me to spin the straw into gold for you this third time?"

"I have nothing left to give you," the maiden said sadly.

"Then promise me," said the little man, "you will give me your first child when you are Queen."

"That may never be," thought the miller's daughter. And as she knew no other way to get her task done, she promised the little man what he asked. Immediately he began to spin.

When the King came in the next morning and found all the room filled with gold, he kept his promise and married the miller's daughter and they lived together happily enough.

With the birth of her first child, the Queen was filled with joy and forgot all about the little man and her promise. One day he came to her chamber and reminded her of it. She was grieved at the thought of giving up her child and offered him all the treasures of the kingdom instead, but she pleaded in vain. The little man did not want treasure.

At last her tears softened him, and he said, "I will give

you three day's grace. If during that time you can tell me my
name, you shall keep your child."

The Queen lay awake all night, thinking of all the names
that she had ever heard. In the morning she dispatched messengers all over the land to inquire of new ones. The next
day, when the little man came, she began with Throckmor-
ton, Florizel, Peramund and all the other unusual names she
could remember. But to all of them he said, "That's not my
name."

The second day she began with all the comical names she
had heard of—Bandy-legs, Pigeon-toes, and the like—but
to every one of them the dwarf still said, "That's not my
name."

The third day one of the messengers came back to report,
"I heard of no other name. But yesterday, as I was climbing
a high hill among the trees of the forest where the fox and
the hare bid each other good night, I saw a little hut, and
before the hut burned a fire, and around the fire a funny little
man danced on one leg, and sang:

> "Today I brew, and then I'll bake,
> Tomorrow the Queen's child I'll take;
> The Queen will never win this game,
> For Rumpelstiltskin is my name."

When the Queen heard this, she jumped for joy.

Soon her little visitor came, and said, "Now, Lady, what
is my name?"

"Is it John?" she asked.

"No!"

"Is it Tom?"

"No!"

"Can your name be Rumpelstiltskin?"

"The witches told you! The witches told you!" shrieked

the little man, and in a rage he stamped his right foot so hard into the floor that he was forced to take hold of it with both hands to pull it out. Off he rushed, and he has never been seen again from that day to this.

Robert j Lee